Fried Rice

A Novel

Leah Hermann

For my loving parents, dedicated husband,

eccentric children, and two best girlfriends.

Acknowledgments

I am thankful for my talented graphic designer, Chi Hom, who created the best romantic comedy novel cover I've ever seen. You truly have been blessed with a genuine gift.

Liane Larocque, thank you for editing my novel, but more so, thank you for pushing me to succeed as an author. Your words of encouragement are priceless, and I'm so grateful to have gotten to know you!

Chapter One

"Breakup"

"Hey, Eva. So… I don't think this relationship is going to work out. Although I really enjoyed our time together… I just think that your personality doesn't meld well with mine, and your lifestyle is quite a bit different. I mean… I'm not really sure I want kids. Might not really be my thing."

Brandi's eyebrows start to become one, gathering in the middle of her forehead. Her ferocity emerges as she finishes reading the "breakup" text from Mike. "Well, that guy is clearly an idiot!" she says, fuming while throwing her arms to the Heavens.

"What does he even mean by '*your* lifestyle?'" Her face scrunches up in annoyance again as her fingers imitate quotes around the words—your lifestyle. "*Clearly*, he is a man-child if he doesn't want kids."

Brandi sees my eyes are starting to glaze over. She relaxes, breathes in deeply, sighs, and hands my phone back. "I'm sorry the online dating thing isn't really taking off like I thought it would for you," she says. "I really didn't think there were that many losers out there."

Brandi sits down next to me on her white, almost pristine, hand-me-down couch that was gifted to her from her parents. My pillow and folded blankets lie neatly on the armrest. Brandi wraps her arm around my shoulder. I flinch as the strands of Brandi's hair graze the side of my face. Her hair still damp from body surfing at the shores all morning. I inhale the sea's aroma, and it reminds me of Liam's and my first date. The best date I had ever been on.

My mind begins to wander. I start to picture myself entangled in Liam's strong arms while we sit on the chilled sand, a result of the sun falling below the horizon a couple hours prior. I sit between his legs, facing the ocean. I slide one of my hands inside the sleeve of his high school basketball hoodie and wrap my hand around his warm wrist. His other hand leaves my waist to block the coastal breeze on my hand that isn't nestled away in his sweater. He kisses the top of my head, and I imagine how his perfect lips would feel on mine. I start to imagine us dancing around our personal bonfire while using sparklers to draw circles and other miscellaneous shapes into the salty air. His amber eyes are entranced by my slender figure that's encased in ripped, faded, skintight jeans that are all the rage with millennials. My thoughts are enveloped by his fanciful smile, which leads me to fixate on his sensual lips again. I start to dream about lying down next to Liam as our fascination with one another explodes. I stare into his exquisite light brown eyes as he gently twists my long auburn hair between his fingers. He puts one of his earbuds in each of our ears, and we momentarily escape from reality while he sings along to his playlist that consists mostly of upbeat teenage heartbreak songs.

Brandi gently gives my shoulder a couple shakes with her hand that's wrapped around my back, and she squeezes me tightly against her sandy shirt, which snaps me back to the present time. "Eva, don't give up. I—"

"Mike *is* an idiot. Brandi, I literally went on two dates with him. Two!" I hold up the number two on my hand for dramatic effect. "There was no need for a breakup text." I rub the back of my neck while staring at my phone. "The first date we went on, I felt bad for the guy."

I begin to explain, "We had just sat down at the table, and when the waitress brought us our menus, I realized he was sweating profusely. His Star Wars shirt was *completely* drenched in sweat, and his dirty blonde hair was two shades darker than his profile picture. His comb-over was plastered down directly onto his head."

"Oh, nooo!" Brandi says. She cracks up. "You mean plastered from all the sweat?"

"Yeah! He reminded me of Pee-wee Herman. Seriously, the grossest thing I've ever seen." A small smile begins to consume my face as I continue, "Before our server took our drink order, she walked over to us and pulled out a gigantic stack of napkins from her apron. She set it right in front of Mike. Then she gave me a quick wink and proceeded to ask what we would like to drink." Brandi covers her grin with her manicured fingertips as I tell her my horror story. "Then I, *for sure*, saw a sweat droplet make its way onto his chicken taco. Needless to say, he devoured his taco plate in the time I took three bites of my burrito. I know I'm a slow eater, but come on! I ate a third of my food and asked for a to-go box. I basically eliminated the awkward presence of me eating by myself for the next half-hour while Mike waded in his kiddie pool of sweat." I started to laugh even harder, thinking about the date.

"Oh, my gosh! What the heck?" Brandi howls as she throws her upper body forward over her tan legs. Her hands fly onto her face, and her back hunches over from laughter. "And, you totally ate the rest of the burrito in your car, *didn't you?*"

"Uh, yeah. I did." We chuckle together.

"Wow, Eva. I really am so sorry you had to deal with that." She is still giggling, but I know she cares and possibly feels bad for me.

"It is what it is," I murmur. "Maybe it's some kind of medical condition? I think I remember someone telling me about people getting shots in their armpits, so they don't sweat as much or something."

The next thing I know, I'm trying to push the image of Mike having sex out of my brain. I fail. Pictures of him panting over some poor girl's body as he attempts to make love to her invade my thoughts. Perspiration envelops his entire body, and globs of sweat collect on Mike's forehead. Marble-sized droplets fall onto the sheets and the desperate girl's face.

I swallow deeply, successfully sending the vomit at the top my throat back to the depths of my stomach, and reply, "I guess it is pretty funny now that the date is over and done with."

"Yeah, friggin' hilarious!" Brandi responds as she slaps my thigh, which is covered by my stained leggings. "I'm really finding it hard to believe you went on a second date with him."

"I know, me too, now that I think about it."

"What made you decide to go on a second date?" Brandi inquires.

"I thought maybe he would be less nervous the second time around and wouldn't sweat so much?" I made an unsure gesture with my pasty white arms.

"Okay." Brandi nods, but she's still skeptical of my answer. "So, how did things go?"

"Well, it gets better." Brandi sits up straight like a toddler waiting for her dessert to be brought to her—anxious and impatient. "So, during our last date at the mini-golf course, he told me he made coconut cream pie and asked if I wanted to try a slice."

"Wait, what?" Brandi leans back and looks at me, confused. "Pie?" She thinks for a moment. "Oh, you told him that's one of your favorites on the date before, yeah?" She was really trying to give Mike the benefit of the doubt.

"Uh, no, I actually did *not* tell him that." The moisture inside my eyes glisten from laughter. "Anyway, I went along with it. I thought he was going to say he could drop off a piece later, which actually made me kind of excited, but then I wasn't sure if I wanted to give him my address. All these insane scenarios were going through my head, and then he grabbed my hand. Like a dog on a leash, he started pulling me toward his beat-up teal sedan. He opened the door to the back seat, and then I was thinking, *am I about to be abducted?*"

Brandi's eyes get wide. "Well, he pulled out a slice of

coconut cream pie that had been sitting on the ripped back seat of his car. The pie wasn't in a container or anything. It was *literally* a slice of coconut cream pie, plated on a white glass plate. He even had forks in the back of his driver's seat."

"Wow, he came prepared." We die from laughter.

"Yeah, tell me about it. Anyway, I was so confused. I just ended up telling him I thought he said *banana* cream pie, and my throat swells up like a pissed-off puffer fish when I eat coconut. Then, I went on and said how I hope my daughter, Genesis, doesn't have any food allergies. You know, to try to make my lie sound legit." I'm a terrible liar and typically feel guilty for weeks after being deceitful.

One time, when I was nine, I lied to my mom about borrowing her razor to shave my entire body. It was a terrible idea. I had to wear pants and long-sleeved shirts for a week and a half in the middle of July until my leg hair grew back. My mom knew the truth but didn't try to contest my dishonesty. Her lull ended up feeding my guilt even more. I had trouble sleeping for days.

"Mike mentioned I never told him I had a daughter. He jumped into his beater car and drove off without saying another word. I think the whole mom thing freaked him out."

Once Brandi has finally recovered from her laughing attack and wipes the tears from her hazel eyes, she replies, "I guess I shouldn't have been so lenient with the age range on your dating profile, like you suggested." Brandi shrugs and says, "You were right, most twenty-two and twenty-three-year-old boys probably aren't ready to raise a princess like Genesis, but I still think you will find someone soon. I should probably add to your profile that you have a little one, just to make sure we avoid all this nonsense from happening again." She's hopeful.

Our conversation is finished prematurely when Genesis wakes up from her afternoon nap. "Oh, Genesis! Did Auntie wake you with all that laughing?" Brandi walks over to Genesis' crib that's parked in her living room, but not before she retrieves her niece's hearing aid. "Auntie Brandi is coming to save you! My beautiful girly!" she says in her best baby voice. "I missed you so much this morning, my love."

Genesis is standing up in her slatted crib as she clings onto the rail for support, awaiting Auntie to release her from baby jail. Genesis' eyes light up, and she replies with a slur of joyful baby gibberish.

Brandi picks up my daughter and places her on the changing table. Genesis challenges Brandi, as she attempts to put the hearing aid in her ear.

Uncoordinated, adorable baby hands slap the air. Brandi reaches for a diaper and leans over to press her nose against Genesis' nose. "Mommy met a dumb boy online, didn't she?" Brandi declares in a low voice while she and Genesis give each other Eskimo kisses.

I walk over to the fridge and pull out a large Tupperware of fried rice I made a day ago. In the last year and a half, I have not broken my roommate agreement—always keep the fridge stocked with five-star meals and never run out of my family's famous fried rice.

The perfect combination of sweet and salty introduces itself into the air as our lunch reheats in the microwave. "Genesis, your mommy must be a mind reader," Brandi exclaims as she buckles my baby girl into the highchair. "Mommy's heating up some num-nums for us, pretty girl. Mmm!"

Genesis and I are blessed to have Brandi in our lives. If it weren't for her love for us, we would be living with my parents, who would, no doubt, remind me every day of their disapproval—their disapproval of my failed relationship with Genesis' father, Liam.

Chapter Two

Brandi Miu Ryan

"Mmm, your favorite Genesis, eggs. You love when Mommy cooks you eggs, huh, my pretty lady?" Genesis nods her head, showing off her toothy smile. She yanks her bright pink hearing aid out of her left ear and throws it on the floor. Genesis smirks at her accomplishment. I pick up her hearing aid and wiggle it back into her ear. I point my finger at her. "Now, you leave that in, baby girl."

"Auntie's home!" Brandi says while dramatically flinging open the door. Her blonde hair is in a long French braid, and she's dressed in lavender scrubs covered in oversized daisies.

"Hi, Auntie. Hi," Genesis says in her soft but high-pitched baby voice.

Brandi ecstatically responds, "Hi, cutie pie!" and waves at Genesis. Genesis waves back. "Now it's time for the *other* baby to get some attention," Brandi says as she picks up her miniature Dachshund, Sasuke. "Aw, I bet you want some yummies too. Doncha', Mr. Wienie? Were you a good boy for Auntie Eva?" She gives Sasuke his morning smooch on his sable fur and a ten-second scratch behind his floppy ears. "No accidents? No barking at nothing? I think Genesis has been giving you too many snacks, my chunky boy."

She gently sets Sasuke down on the floor. The overweight wiener waddles to his doggy bed nestled next to Genesis' and my overflowing, free-standing rack of clothes. Sasuke stays in his bed for a brief moment, jumps up, and waddles over next to Genesis' highchair to vacuum up snacks the little princess has thrown. Brandi walks over to Genesis and gives her a peck on her rosy, chubby cheek. Genesis giggles and coos at the same time, enjoying the affection she's receiving from her auntie.

I smile, thinking about how Sasuke means "warrior" in Japanese.

I looked the meaning up on the internet when Brandi first named him, just like I did in high school to learn the meaning of Brandi's middle name. I realized her middle name wasn't a typical name for someone who is Caucasian. It turned out that Mr. and Mrs. Ryan were big fans of anime. I guess Miu was a character in some adult cartoon they liked.

Every time I would refer to anime as an "adult cartoon," a disgusted look developed on Brandi's face. She told me multiple times to stop calling it that, but I didn't and still don't listen. She says it makes it sound like animated porno. But really... am I wrong? No one can deny the fact that in every anime there is always at least one character with humongous boobs—at least one chick, if not more, wearing basically nothing. At least, that was the case in the animes that Liam always used to watch. Whenever I cooked dinner, Liam would be fixated on some anime on TV. Every now and then, I would pause from cooking and glance up at the screen, only to find him watching some big-boobied cartoon character on the television.

"Sasuke was a good boy," I tell Brandi. I lean over and pat Sasuke on his head. "But he didn't want to go potty while it was raining. Still, deathly afraid of a little water, aren't you, Sasuke? He just peed in the house once, in his favorite spot, by the front door."

"Mister Wiener! Do I need to get you a doggy diaper?" Brandi says, joking. "Luckily, it doesn't rain too often in San Diego, or you would *definitely* be wearing one of those doggy diapers." Brandi chuckles to herself.

Fried Rice

Brandi and Sasuke have lived in their modern townhome for the last six years or so. It comes with a decent-sized yard for Sasuke. However, he doesn't do much running around unless it's to scavenge for tidbits which sums up the extent of his daily exercise.

Brandi always tells me how lucky she is that her parents helped her with the down payment for her beautiful townhome. Since she was studying so hard for her nursing career, her parents agreed to help. She's so thankful, but her dream has always been to live on the beach.

I recall her saying, "I just want to be able to wake up with the sunrise and run into the waves whenever I feel like it." She basically has an identical heart to baby Moana's.

Her townhome is also a museum that consists of beach artwork—a home that is complete with coastal-style furniture. My favorites are the wooden tiki man by the door and, secretly, the painting I made for her birthday last year. The floor tile reminds me of long planks of beach driftwood. Her kitchen is lined with bright white cabinets, and a small green island resides in the middle of her open kitchen. It matches the shelves that line the window above the large farm sink. I told Brandi her home looked like something straight out of an episode of *House and Garden*. When I first moved in, I told her she could've been an interior designer, but really, I already knew she wanted to follow in her mom's footsteps. That's why she became an RN.

"How was work last night?" I ask Brandi as I plate her breakfast—eggs, bacon, and a fresh blueberry muffin I made from scratch.

"Busy as usual," she beams. "Oh! I actually need to shower... *like now!*" She walks quickly toward the bathroom. "One of my patients smeared poop all over his sheets. It smelled—"

"No more details!" I yell from the kitchen as I cringe at the thought of having to change an adult's poopy sheets. Genesis' baby poops are bad enough.

"Yeahhh, yeahhh!" she yells back. I know she's laughing at me again.

"Your breakfast is in the microwave," I shout.

Brandi doesn't respond. She is already in the shower, happily singing the lyrics to some country love song about tequila. She is still shining brightly, even after enduring a rough night at the hospital. She always amazes me. I think to myself, once again, how it truly takes a strong person with a big heart to be a nurse.

I've known Brandi since the beginning of high school. She's always had a beautiful soul. She never hesitated to help someone in need. One sunny day, I was walking to fourth period. I spotted Brandi comforting one of our classmates who was alone, crying by the girl's locker room. I'm pretty sure the girl's name was Alice.

Alice had her back pushed up against the stone exterior of the building, and her knees were pressed tightly against her chest. The poor thing was bawling her pretty blue eyes out. She was probably upset over a silly teen breakup. The kind of breakup we laugh about after we go on a date with a new interest, simply forgetting the past relationship that only lasted weeks or maybe months.

Brandi sat down beside Alice and scooted close to the isolated girl. Brandi gently leaned her head against the side of Alice's head to let her know she wasn't alone. Brandi rambled something into Alice's ear, and I saw them giggle. Whatever she said also produced a slanted smile on Alice's face, but then she quickly went back to crying. I saw Brandi take her thumb and try to swipe at the tears that streamed down Alice's flushed cheeks.

Brandi continued to sit with Alice as I went on my way to class. Plenty of students walked by but didn't care to stop and console Alice like Brandi did. Brandi didn't even care about the copious amounts of snot that came pouring down Alice's face. I've known Brandi's true character from the beginning of our friendship, but after hearing one too many details about her nursing job, I started to see her loving heart even more vividly.

Chapter Three

Blessings

"What a blessing," Liam's mom said when I told her we were expecting.

It was hard to believe that she actually meant it. She looked shocked when I told her I was four months pregnant, and then she abruptly turned to Liam's father and spattered something into his ear.

I had been nagging Liam to tell his parents about the baby for a long time. I reminded him daily, for a month straight, after I found out I was pregnant, but he never got around to breaking the good news to anyone. He said it was never the right time.

Finally, after more weeks went by, I decided I would tell his parents on my own. I thought it would be a great time during his mom's 51st birthday dinner. I thought it would be a nice present for her. I thought she would be excited to be a grandma.

Not only was Liam furious, but apparently, I ruined his mom's birthday too.

"Why would you do that? I clearly said I wanted to wait to tell them," Liam said irritably as we walked to the car. "I don't know why you never listen to me."

I wrapped my tan coat around my waist and looked around his parents' neighborhood to see if anyone was standing outside. I sighed with relief. No one heard Liam lecturing me.

Once we were seated in Liam's hatchback, he quickly started the car and turned the volume on the radio all the way down. I noticed his grip on the steering wheel as he accelerated. His fists became tighter and tighter, like a rock climber over-gripping his holds. I could feel each individual heartbeat in my chest and pain welling up in my eyes. He was about to continue his lecture, but I turned to face him and cut him off.

"I'm going to be showing soon anyway. I mean, I kind of look like I have a small baby bump already, and I've been asking you to tell your mom and dad for the last... how many weeks?"

"You didn't need to do it on my mom's birthday," he said, staring straight ahead at the red light overhead.

"Well, when would have been a better time for *you*?" I asked as tears fell from my eyes. My voice became more intense. "Are your parents upset because we didn't get married first or maybe because you haven't fully started your career yet? I don't understand." I wiped my nose on the sleeve of my coat and crossed my arms. I felt alone, like Alice. "I really thought they would be excited, but I guess—"

Now it was Liam's turn to interrupt me. He reached for the volume knob and turned the music louder than it originally had been when we first sat down in his car. That was fine. I already knew the answers to my questions. There was no need for Liam to respond. We were silent the rest of the car ride home. I stared out the window, continuing to wipe the frustration and hurt away on the collar of my coat. I tried to look at the sky, but the stars were just blurry specks. I shut my eyes for a minute and started to say a silent prayer. It seemed to always help me feel more at ease and hopeful whenever Liam and I got into an argument.

When we walked through the gray door to our apartment, I tried to apologize. I set my purse down on the antique chair we purchased at the thrift store last spring. I quickly followed behind him, like a dog following his master, as he headed toward our bedroom. I reached for his hand, hoping he would allow me to see his face, but he immediately snapped his hand away from my grasp like it was a dangerous rat trap.

"I'm sorry I told your parents about the good news." Liam paused and stood in place to hear me out, but he still didn't turn around to look me in the eyes.

I continued with my apology, "I didn't mean to upset anyone, especially on your mom's birthday. I now realize I should've waited until we both agreed to tell them together." I said this through my teeth, but it was sincere, nonetheless.

Liam mumbled to himself sarcastically, *"Good news? What good news?"*

My chest felt like a rubber band stretched to its limit. Then, Liam paused and looked over his shoulder as if he might lecture me again for the third time tonight. Instead, he turned his head back around and stormed off to the bedroom. He reminded me of the Hulk, a scrawnier version of the Hulk, a *much* scrawnier version.

Liam was never one for talking things out or admitting he was wrong. I always thought it was an Asian trait. Most Asian men don't like to talk about their feelings, and they are right about anything and everything, no questions asked or else!

I think I've seen my dad apologize to my mom less than three times in the twenty-eight years that I've been alive. The only time I fully remember details of my dad apologizing to my mom was when my dad had kissed some lady on her neck. We were at some type of gathering with family and friends, someone's house I wasn't too familiar with. I was only six or seven at the time.

My dad committed a horrible act in front of my mom and more than half of the people at the party. I looked at my mom, tugging on her blouse, and asked her why Daddy was kissing that lady over there. I looked up at her, impatiently waiting for an answer. My mom's eyes filled with tears, but she quickly managed to hold them back; she noticed the sets of eyes in the room were now focused on her. She began to laugh along with my dad and the random lady at the party, like it was no big deal her husband had just kissed another lady's neck.

I think my dad had genuine and playful intentions. He probably thought he was "messing around" or something. He probably thought he was being funny, but he clearly wasn't thinking at all. My dad wasn't thinking of the consequences of how his hurtful actions would enrage his wife.

He tilted the random lady over his knee, like they do in ballroom dances and sucked on her neck for a couple seconds. A couple seconds too long. The unattractive lady should've been replaced by the most beautiful woman at the party, my mom. He should have been kissing his wife's neck and not the lady's.

When we got home from the party, my mom was outraged. I don't think I'd ever seen her more hurt and angry than I did that day. She began yelling at my dad, telling him how it was wrong that he kissed someone else, even if it was meant to be silly. She explained to him how embarrassed she had been when everyone stared at her to see what reaction she had from witnessing her husband kiss another woman.

I started to cry at the sight of my parents ferociously fighting in the middle of our living room. After ten minutes of back and forth yelling, my dad eventually apologized, realizing his mistake. He wasn't used to confrontation with my mom. She usually bit her tongue, always careful to pick and choose her fights wisely.

I watched as my dad tilted my mom over his knee and kissed her neck, just like he had previously done at the party with someone else, but his kiss lingered a while longer. My mom giggled as my dad picked her up like newlyweds do when the husband carries his wife over the threshold. He proceeded to carry her into their bedroom upstairs. My crying stopped; I was thankful the argument between my parents had finally come to an end.

My dad slammed the door shut to their room. I knew this meant it was Mommy and Daddy's "private" time. I went into my room and started to play with my

Barbie dolls. I grabbed my Ken doll in one hand and Barbie in the other. I began to play out a scene where Ken makes out with Barbie on her neck.

Four days after our fight, Liam told me he didn't want to ruin his future, and he was leaving me... us. I really didn't have much to say. My head and heart felt like they were encased in ice. I looked down at my belly and rubbed my baby bump, thinking about my baby girl growing up fatherless.

I was positive I couldn't change his mind, and it's hard when someone doesn't want you. I didn't want to *ruin* his future.

He ended up moving back in with his parents. I think they were happy because they were never delighted in the first place when we told them we had applied to get an apartment together.

"Couples who aren't married shouldn't move in with one another." Liam's mom began to shame us. "It's not right in the eyes of God." I felt like I was thirteen again and had done something naughty to upset Liam's mom.

I suppose I couldn't blame her. After all, my parents felt the same way about Liam's and my living situation. Deep down, I knew my mom and dad only wanted the best for me, emotionally and financially. They always told me it was best to do things in order—date, marry, house, babies.

I, obviously, did not follow their instructions, and if moving in before marriage wasn't bad enough in both our parents' eyes, having a baby out of wedlock is frowned upon even more. It seemed to be culturally taboo.

I remember when I first started dating James during my freshman year of high school, the first boyfriend I ever had. My mom wanted to have "the talk" with me.

"I just want to make sure you are being safe, if you decide to have sex."

"Mom, do we have to talk about this?" I said, embarrassed.

"I don't want you to ruin your future," she explained.

"I know. I understand," I said, trying to end the awkward conversation.

"Date, marriage, house, kids—in that order, but I know that sometimes teenagers don't listen to their parents' advice," she told me as I avoided eye contact.

"James and I haven't even kissed. I don't think you need to worry," I reassured her.

"Well, if and when you decide to have sex, you need to make sure you—"

"Mom, please don't say what I think you are about to say."

"Take birth control, even if you use a condom," she continued.

Phew, she didn't say double-bag it. "Okay, I will Mom. Can we be done now?"

"Yes, but just know, I only want the best for you."

Sometimes, I think I should've listened to my mom and dad when I look at my checking account or think of my situation with Genesis' non-existent father, but then I remember how much joy Genesis has brought into my life. I never knew I could love someone so much until the first day she was born.

Anyway, I guess I shouldn't have convinced myself my parents would approve of us living together during my junior year of college, just because Liam was the Asian boyfriend my dad had been waiting for.

Chapter Four

Mr. & Mrs. Gin

I'm still not one hundred percent sure why my dad wasn't interested in my "non-Asian" boyfriends. During the middle of my freshman year, I introduced my dad to James. James was always polite, but I don't think my dad said more than two sentences to James the three weeks we were dating.

The first time he met my dad, James walked over to him in the living room. James smiled awkwardly. "Nice to meet you, Mr. Gin." He gave a small wave toward my dad, followed by a nervous chortle. My dad sat sleepily on the couch. He tended to do this a lot on his weekends, usually after lunch. Sometimes, I would catch him grumbling to himself about when he would finally be able to retire from the office job he despised so much.

"Two more years until retirement. One and a half more years until retirement," he would say, squinting at the television.

Also, my parents weren't all that young. They had me later in life, something which, surprisingly, turned out to be nice because they were able to really provide for me.

Throughout my childhood, my dad would bring home dim sum twice a month, maybe more if he was feeling generous. The fried dumplings and pork-filled buns were, and still are, some of my favorite foods. I suppose my six-year-old friends would've preferred chicken nuggets and fries, but I was the exception. He would always try to surprise me when he came home after work. I would sprint to the door as fast as Sasuke runs to Genesis' highchair, ready to devour the delicious cuisine my dad held in his hands.

This was when I realized *food is a form of love.*

"Dad, this is James," I said, a feeble attempt to avert his gaze from the movie.

My dad broke eye contact from the TV for a split second, but not because I said something. I think James' overly preppy outfit might've caught my dad's eye for a split second. I thought he might say, "Nice to meet you too, James," but instead, my dad had a blank expression spewed across his face.

"You play golf?" my dad asked.

"Oh, no," James chuckled as he smoothed out his gray polo shirt. "I swim," he explained nervously and tucked his hands into his preppy golfer shorts. "I'm also on the dive team." James continued to fail, trying to get my dad's attention.

James flinched at the screams coming from the 80s horror movie my dad had playing in the background. He turned toward the TV and saw a possessed doll with crazy, bright red hair run across the screen. Clearly, James was not comfortable at all. He combed his fingers through his parted hair, his shiny brunette hair that looked as if it might've had a touch too much hair gel.

"Hmm," my dad turned back toward his 70" TV and continued watching *Child's Play* as if James no longer stood next to him.

My dad wasn't the first one to lose interest in James' and my relationship.

"What the heck, Eva? Just eat lunch with us on the grass. James can join us too," Brandi said, adjusting her gold bow that was tied around her high ponytail on the top of her head.

Brandi and I must've had our first "argument" on a Friday because I remembered Brandi wearing her cheerleading uniform. She looked adorable in her royal blue skirt and skintight top that read GHS. Unlike my body, Brandi's was super athletic. I just got lucky; my parents graciously passed down their fast metabolism genes to me. The uniform fit Brandi perfectly on her perfect Barbie body.

"James says there's not enough shade or whatever." I tried to justify what I was explaining. "He says the bench area covered by trees is a perfect spot for lunch. That's why he and his friends like to hang out there."

"Well, maybe James should trade in those polos he wears every day for a tank or a normal shirt. Then he wouldn't complain so much." Brandi gently scratched her temple as she looked down at the ground. She instantly regretted judging James for how he dressed. The following three weeks were strange for the both of us, sitting next to one another in art class wasn't what it had normally been.

Three weeks later, James threw in the towel. "I don't think your dad likes me very much," he said, embarrassed. "I feel bad..." he explained while running his hand down the front of his shirt.

Apparently, he did that when he was in an uncomfortable situation. "It was cool chillin' with you these last three weeks though." James looked at the dirt as he said, "I still think you are the most beautiful girl in the school."

I'm pretty sure he was just trying to be polite again. It made me second-guess if he was being honest when he used to say he thought my eyes were transcending. So annoying.

"It's okay. I understand. Sorry he didn't warm up to you," I replied.

I walked away from James, not all that surprised by our breakup, and purchased a slice of cheese pizza at the lunch window. Then, I headed over to the grass area to try to apologize to Brandi, someone who sincerely cared about me. I thought of James' stupid polos and crusty hair as I spotted Brandi in the distance.

It was fine. No big deal. I tried to persuade myself into thinking I hadn't lost a valuable relationship with James.

I remember the one and only time he called to talk to me. I think he was afraid my dad would pick up the phone before I did if he attempted to call the house phone.

"Oh, uh, hi, Mr. Gin. Good evening. Is Eva available?"

"Who is this? Jim?" my dad said, confident in his guess.

"Um, yes, sir—James, this is James. I just had a quick question about a group project that I need to ask Eva about. I promise I won't keep her up too late."

Fried Rice

My dad handed me the phone. "It's Jim," he said in his normal, deep, grumpy voice.

"Hi, Jim!" I say, jokingly.

James sounded panicked. "Eva! Why didn't you answer your cell? Your dad scares the crap out of me. I mean... I'm sorry, I didn't mean that." I turned the speaker on the phone away from my mouth and tried not to laugh too loudly.

I also think James and I only held hands twice, maybe three times. I can't recall, but I didn't mind because his hands were always clammy, like a baby's butt locked up too long in a diaper. I really had a thing about sweaty boys, easily grossed out I suppose. I always tried to be sneaky and wipe my hand on my clothes after our hand-holding session. I didn't want to hurt Mr. Polite's feelings.

As I approached Brandi and her other friends eating lunch, I saw her half-smile and wave at me. She sprung up from her seat on the grass and jogged toward me. She greeted me with a sisterly hug. We sat down and enjoyed our overdue lunch date together under the California sunshine.

"I'm over it," I told Brandi. I pulled out my Tupperware of lukewarm fried rice my mom cooked for dinner the night before. I handed Brandi the small container of fried rice and proceeded to eat my slice of pizza.

She gasped sarcastically, "For me?" Her face lit up as she tossed her half-eaten cheeseburger down and began eating her favorite dish without hesitation.

This was when I learned *food is a form of apology.*

"Lots of fishies in the sea," she replied. She shot me a sympathetic laugh before taking a monstrous bite of fried rice. "But, next time, hook one that can soak up the rays with us while we eat lunch," she said, sarcastically while reaching her long arms out, toward the light blue sky—the container still in one hand and a spoon in the other. She closed her eyes and smiled at the clouds. I think she was imagining herself sitting on the beach.

Yes, there were lots of fishies in the sea, hence, my sophomore boyfriend, Thomas. I thought I would get some type of reaction out of my dad when I brought Thomas over to the house. I really thought my dad was going to enjoy Thomas' company like I did, but my assumptions were wrong. So wrong. Again.

During dinner with my parents, Thomas bragged about his uncle being a surgeon and his older brother being a paramedic. "I definitely want my career to be in the medical field too. I want to make my parents proud," he claimed.

"Mmm," my dad responded and continued to slurp down the winter melon soup my mom made for dinner.

Later that evening, Thomas texted me and asked what was in the soup we had for dinner. He had graciously eaten three bowls of the winter melon soup. It's hard to say no when Mrs. Gin keeps refilling your bowl without consent. At least my mom liked him. Each time Thomas cleaned his bowl, she smirked like she was about to beat her girlfriends at a game of Mahjong.

A couple months into dating Thomas, my mom randomly said to me, "You know, if you have babies with Thomas, they are going to be really big. If you have babies with an Asian guy, they will be a lot smaller." I was dumbfounded and shocked my mom said this. I'm not really sure what expression I had on my face at the time, but my mom's face remained confident, like she was telling me a hard fact. I stood there, waiting for a more thorough explanation, but my mom began laughing uncontrollably after she heard some dirty joke that came from the TV. My confusion was directed elsewhere.

"*Role Models?*" I asked, surprised. "Mom!" I began to laugh along with her.

"Oh my goodness," my mom said, catching her breath as she grabbed at the neckline of her ivory floral shirt.

"This movie *is* pretty hilarious," I said as I sat down next to my mom. I rested my head on her shoulder while watching her crochet a beanie for my dad. The crimson yarn intertwined around her fingers. Every now and then, she would bust up laughing at the movie. I would join in too, but I was mostly laughing because she was laughing.

Chapter Five

Asian Persuasion

Liam came over for dinner at the beginning of my senior year of high school. As soon as Liam walked through my parents' door, my dad rushed over to meet him. My dad took Liam's hand in both of his and aggressively shook it. The greeting between my dad and Liam seemed to last an entire minute.

"Hi, Mr. Gin. It's such a pleasure to meet you and your wife. Thank you for having me over for dinner. Eva's told me so many good things about you." Brown-nosing had always been Liam's forte.

My dad had the biggest grin on his face. It reminded me of when he hit the thousand-dollar jackpot at the casino. It might have been an even larger grin. He looked like the Joker from *Batman*. I stood next to my gawking dad, completely in shock.

Then, I realized Liam was getting the "Asian approval" from my dad. Yup, my dad finally showed interest in one of my boyfriends. The Asian one.

I remembered my dad telling me about how his parents met. My grandpa never laid eyes on his soon-to-be wife until she stepped off the bus. My grandpa had been sent from the States back to China to become educated. When his education was complete, he eventually was set up with a wife. She would accompany him back to the U.S., where he would work in my great-grandpa's liquor store, somewhere in the heart of Los Angeles.

My grandpa arrived at the bus stop an hour too early. Impatiently, he sat on the bench, wearing his nicest pair of pants and button-up shirt, as he waited for the bus my grandma was traveling on to arrive.

Apprehensively, he thought to himself, I hope the matchmaker didn't set me up with someone who is too tall.

Finally, a bus pulled up twenty feet away from him. The bus read *China Bus Company* with Chinese characters printed below. He nervously looked at the farm scenery around him as passengers began to disembark from the two-story bus. Three months of negotiations between my great-grandparents trickled by slower than water dripping from a leaky faucet. The dowry had to be sufficient.

My grandma stepped off the bus in a beautiful, crimson Chinese dress. Her dress was laced with elegant, gold embroidery. Slits on the dress lined both sides of her delicate legs. My grandpa's eyes were abruptly averted from the vegetable farms. He stared at her gorgeous, handmade outfit. She was accompanied by their matchmaker, who guided her to my grandpa. My grandpa looked at my grandma's shoes. Oh, I guess they decided not to bind her feet. *That's okay*, my grandpa thought to himself. At least, she's not taller than I am, and that's what's important.

After high school, Liam's goal was to get into the medical field or, maybe, it was his parents' goal. Either way, Liam had just started his paid internship at one of the main hospitals in San Diego when I became pregnant. He was on his way to becoming a pharmacist.

We agreed he was going to be our main source of income, and I could stick to working part-time at the cafe as long as I was willing to complete all the housework. Obviously, that plan went to crap.

Chapter Six

Home

I knew that budgeting would be even harder once I had a newborn. I wasn't sure how I was going to be able to afford the rent by myself while working at Janette's Cafe. Even with any extra hours I could possibly pick up, and the free childcare provided by my parents and Brandi, I still didn't think it would be possible. I started to think that I would have to move back in with my parents like Liam did with his. My love for my mom and dad was endless, but the thought of seeing and hearing their disappointment day after day would eventually take its toll.

When I told Brandi about me "ruining" Liam's future, she didn't hesitate to offer her home to us. She actually apologized multiple times for not having a spare room, but we could stay as long as we needed or wanted to. I told her I couldn't possibly be a burden, especially with a newborn on the way. Of course, Brandi kept on insisting.

"You can keep Sasuke company. He's home all night by himself when I have to go to work. He would love it. I would love it." Brandi continued, "Plus, your cooking! Yes! I would basically be taking advantage of every one of your delicious meals."

"I don't know… After the baby gets here, the crying will probably keep you up. You won't get any sleep, and…"

"Don't worry about it. I will get earplugs if I need to. Everything will be fine. I want to spend time with my gorgeous niece. Please! And I need your fried rice daily."

My grandma had passed down an amazing fried rice recipe to my mom, and my mom had gladly taught me how to make our famous family dish when I was just ten years old. I remember her allowing me to finally hold a knife in my hand, entrusting me to carefully cut the ingredients. I remember her allowing me to turn on the burner to the stove, entrusting me to safely cook our family meal.

This was when I realized *food is a form of the past.*

One day, I will entrust Genesis with our family's sacred fried rice recipe, just as my mom has done with me. I hope Genesis will never forget the day when I show her how to make fried rice. I hope, when Genesis has kids of her own, she will pass the knowledge on to them and so on.

I couldn't argue with Brandi any longer. Weeks before Genesis was born, Brandi helped me set up her changing table and crib across from my couch bed. She surprised me with an early baby shower gift—a sea-themed bouncer which looked like a planned-out piece in her beach-themed townhome. This was officially *our* home.

Chapter Seven

Profile

"It's been over a year," Brandi huffed. "You are letting me make you this profile!"

Brandi typed away on the laptop like a college student on Adderall, trying to finish her final exam before the deadline. I'm not sure I'd seen Brandi this focused in a while.

"You know, this is how Max and I met. It really works," she tried to assure me.

"I don't want to have to go on a bazillion dates to find Mr. Right. Plus, I've heard some weird stuff about online dating. Like… people message you, asking if you want to do a threesome and crazy stuff like that." My eyeballs started to bulge when I began to think of the messages I would be getting. "I'm getting the willies just thinking about it," I told her.

"It works, Eva! Trust me. You will find someone." She was so sure of herself.

"I dunno..." I said and mentioned the age range, but Brandi ignored my suggestion. "So anyway, do you see yourself marrying Max? I feel like it was a one in a billion chance he happened to be a nurse too."

"I mean, maybe? It's too soon to tell. It's been what, like three months? I don't want to think about it. I just want to enjoy the relationship in the now."

"You got lucky. I'm pretty sure people who participate in online dating have to go on multiple dates with multiple weirdos and filter through multiple, super pervy messages... before finally finding someone. That is, if they ever find someone."

"Okay, negative Nancy," she said in a grumbled voice. "I know I got lucky. It was fun dating here and there in high school and in college. I had no idea it was going to be so hard to find someone who had marriage potential. Plus, life gets in the way, ya know?"

"So, that's a yes?" I asked with a hint of excitement.

"Yes, what?" She was distracted, giving my profile a final look-over.

"*Yes*, you can see yourself marrying Max?"

"Yeah, I suppose. I just don't want to get my hopes up this soon. There—all done!" Brandi clasped her hands together below her chin and started to clap real fast while making high-pitched squealing noises.

Genesis sat on my lap with her musical toy phone and started to laugh and clap her hands along with Brandi. Genesis' big, dark brown eyes lit up as Brandi said, "See Eva, Genesis agrees. Your profile is awesome!"

Chapter Eight

Foot Long

"Can I please have a foot-long, with ham on honey oat? Double meat, please. Oh, and bacon too." I stand, less than enthused, in line at the local sub house.

This afternoon I traded my stained leggings for a Hawaiian print romper. I replaced my messy bun for natural-looking beach waves and exchanged bare feet with a pair of new flip-flops.

My date shuffles down the deli counter behind me. He is overly infatuated with the case that's stocked with various toppings. "I will have the salad," he says as he steps on the backside of my brand new flip-flop, clipping the side of my heel in the process.

"Owww!" I squeal.

"Oh, I'm so, so sorry!" Aaron frantically responds. He places his hand on the top of my shoulder. "Are you okay?"

My mouth is pinched tight, and my hand is covering my heel that had just been stomped on by a ginormous giant. "Yeah, I'm good." No, dummy, No! I am *not* good. "Yeah, it's fine," I lie.

And here we go again! I glance at my purplish-reddish heel and then at his emerald green, baggy capri pants. I'm pretty sure that's what they are called. His pants look more like a potato sack. Cut some holes in the bottom of a sack, stick your legs through, tie it off at the waist, and—WHA BAM! a pair of baggy capri pants.

I wonder if he needs extra space between his crotch and the floor for a specific reason. I start to successfully imagine him having a large—

"Cucumbers?" the girl behind the counter asks.

"Huh?" My eyes shoot up. I redirect my glance from Aaron's crotch to the girl behind the counter. "Oh, yes please," I respond. My face is a little flushed from my X-rated thoughts.

We sit down at the table outside the sub shop. The view isn't all that spectacular. Cars bustle on the busy main road, and there's a couple sitting in a minivan parked in front of us, having a fiery argument with their windows rolled down. I squint at the sun, hoping my fair skin doesn't get roasted like a turkey leg at the fair.

"It's a nice day today," I say to Aaron. He nods

multiple times as he daintily takes a bite of his salad. *Who orders salad at a sandwich shop anyway?* I ask myself.

"The veggies are always so fresh here," he mentions while completely ignoring my lame comment about the weather.

His meatless salad looks more than unappealing. "Are you a vegetarian?" I ask.

"Yeah, you must've read that on my profile. Olives are my favorite fruit. Yeah, and eggplant is my favorite vegetable."

Fruit? I always thought olives were a vegetable. I make a mental note to look that fact up later tonight. He is a professional vegetarian, so I guess he should know. Plus, I've always thought olives were disgusting. They make me gag when I eat them—something weird about the oily, mushy texture.

I rub my bruised foot that's tucked under the metal chair I'm sitting on. "Oh yeah, that's right, I... I, uh, read about you being a vegetarian on your profile," I lie again. Why am I always lying so much on these dates? *I am becoming a sociopath*, I think to myself, yet it's clearly an exaggeration.

"I agree. It's a much healthier option," I say, unsure of my statement. I spent all of sixty seconds looking over his online profile before agreeing to his lunch date. My mistake.

Fried Rice

*****

It had been thirteen days since my last date with Mr. Sweats-a-lot. Brandi had been keeping one of those magnetic whiteboards on the fridge. She thinks it motivates me somehow. Brandi continuously reminds me of my lack of persistence. "You're going to miss out on all the good ones!" she says. Good ones meaning—guys who exude marriage potential qualities.

Every dateless day earns me a tally mark on the whiteboard. Each time I enter the kitchen, it taunts me. It reminds me of the prison cells at Alcatraz when Liam and I visited San Francisco to celebrate our first year as boyfriend and girlfriend. It reminds me of how I will have to filter through my overflowing inbox of debauched messages.

"I didn't become a vegetarian because it's healthier," he explains. "Have you ever seen a pig get slaughtered?"

"I, um, well I—"

"Last year, I stopped eating meat after watching this one movie."

I try to think of what movie would drive a person to become a vegetarian, but I can't think of one off the top of my head. "So, what movie encouraged you to become—"

"The movie with the pig and the spider that can

spell."

"What? You think that's a sad—"

"It's so sad. So, so, so sad. Luckily, the spider saves the pig at the end." He over exaggerates and makes a big frowny face. His lips are puffed out like two fluffy, unappetizing marshmallows.

Now I'm really confused because this guy makes no sense. Also, he keeps on interrupting me! What the hell?

He tucks his loose strand of hair back into his man bun; I don't recall noticing this hairdo on his profile picture. I don't like it.

"I see," I reply back.

I unwrap my foot-long sub and take a heaping bite out of my sandwich. Some pieces of lettuce, along with a slice of bacon, slide out of my sub and onto my tray. Aaron sets his plastic fork down and stares at the crispy strip of bacon. It offends him.

I slowly pick up the delicious piece of bacon and shove it into my mouth. Aaron's eyes are following my every move. "The *meat* is really fresh too," I say passive-aggressively, without a hint of shame.

I know there would, most definitely, *not* be a second date with Aaron.

I start to imagine cooking Aaron dinners. I sort through my mental file of my family's recipes—one vegetable side dish with white sauce. Yeah... this isn't going to work out.

I picture Aaron attending dinner at my parents' house. Aaron offending my mom. Aaron dishonoring her family's fried rice by eating only half of the ingredients in the perfected recipe that had been passed down multiple generations. Aaron leaving all the "slaughtered" meat at the bottom of his bowl.

I wrap up my half-eaten sandwich and begin to fabricate an exit plan.

Aaron recovers, begins picking at his lifeless salad again, and says, "I'm a Water Quality Technician. I've been working with the same company for thirteen years now."

Aaron won't quit rambling on about himself, and I feel like I'm a hiring manager in an interview.

"This year, for my annual raise, they gave me six cents which is double from the year before. I was so stoked. Raises are based on performance. So, I think the company really likes me. I also got employee of the month, like, three years ago. I'm pretty confident that I might get it again next month. There's like, twenty-three employees. So, you know, it's pretty hard to get employee of the month."

"Cool?" I respond, confused again. I'm over it.

"When I'm not working, I like to go to the community garden over by—"

I hastily stand up and grab my sandwich and purse. "Cool! Okay, well, it was nice meeting you. Thanks for the foot-long"—I shake my head real fast—"I mean, lunch. Thank you for the lunch. But I, uh, I just realized I scheduled an appointment... to... get my eyebrows waxed." Dammit, another failed lie.

I speed walk to my lime green Honda with my eyes focused on the ground.

As I'm about to pull out of the parking spot, I notice Aaron trying to yell something at me. I push on the brakes, roll down the window, and stick my head out.

"What was that?" I yell.

He stands up and walks over to the driver's side of my car, abandoning his gross salad.

"Oh, I was just saying that green is my favorite color too."

You *cannot* be serious! Aaron is still trying to have a conversation with me.

He continues, "It reminds me of the grass and leaves on the trees. My whole closet is filled with green shirts and capri pants. Also, I—"

"Okay, uh… BYE!" I yell.

I finally pull out of the parking spot. I look back through the rear window and see Aaron still standing in the same spot. He's waving bye to the back end of my car as I speed off. Another freakishly weird date to add to my resume.

As I sit at a red light, I realize I have just done the same thing Mike had done to me on our last date, maybe worse. I shrug. "Oh well, at least I won't be ridiculed by the whiteboard today!" I say confidently to myself. I unwrap what's left of my lunch and savor every last bite of my delicious ham sandwich while I drive home.

I walk through the door to find Genesis giggling happily in her bouncer. She is currently being entertained by her Auntie. Brandi has her hot pink yoga mat rolled out along the floor. She mimics the poses on the video streaming from her phone.

"How'd it go?" Brandi asks while pressing her hips into downward dog.

"I feel like I wasted an hour of my life."

"Oh, what happened this time?" she asks.

"He kept interrupting me and wouldn't stop talking about himself," I explain. "And he was wearing weird pants."

"You didn't like his pants?" Brandi chortles as she changes her position to upward dog.

"He also had a man bun."

Brandi pauses her video and sits crossed-legged on the mat. She looks at me sternly and says, "Man buns are in! Male models rock that shit."

I shake my head and roll my eyes at her comment. "Hey! You didn't erase my tallies!" I shoot Brandi an evil glance.

Brandi laughs. "Oh, yeah, but tomorrow it starts again!" I use my palm as an eraser and vigorously wipe the whiteboard clean. Brandi presses play on her phone and starts up her video again. "You'll get 'em next time," she says, assured of herself.

The next thing I know, I find myself in the kitchen. I begin gathering the ingredients to make another batch of fried rice, and I try to decide if I'm more disappointed in myself for the way I acted at lunch or more disappointed with the struggles I've been enduring to find Mr. Right.

I start the rice cooker, peel the carrots, and begin cutting up the rest of the ingredients. I hold the dried Chinese sausage on my bamboo cutting board and begin to slice the meat. This has always been my favorite part of making fried rice because it consistently reminds me of my grandma on my mom's side of the family.

She had the most beautiful, long, jet-black hair, just like my father's mom did, but unlike my grandma on my dad's side, Grandma Mary would almost always have her hair pulled back in a low bun. Whenever we visited, she would ask me to style her hair back into a lengthy braid.

Fried Rice

Even when her hair was braided, it still reached the bottom of her hips.

I always thought she was the perfect height for a Chinese woman. Most of us Chinese women look like little people who need a step stool for almost everything. (I can never reach anything on the top shelves in Brandi's kitchen. It's so frustrating). My grandma wasn't just beautiful; she was a hard worker too. My mom was one of nine children. How do you even feed a family that large?

I start to picture the farm my mother lived on as a child. My mom told me the three years she lived on her grandparents' farm were the best days of her childhood. She recalled one day on the farm in Mississippi, telling her mom she wanted a duck for dinner that night.

My grandma told her, "If you want a duck for dinner tonight, you need to go kill it yourself."

My grandma handed my mom the ax, and she hesitantly went outside to behead the duck. She was only around eight or nine at the time, and this was my mother's first time retrieving dinner. She uncoordinatedly swung the ax at the duck's neck. The next thing my mom saw was the duck frantically running around the front yard in the dirt with his head hanging over its neck, like a soggy noodle.

My mom ran back inside the house screaming. Tears were rolling down the front of her cheeks. "Mom! It won't die! It won't die!" she said, terrified. My grandma removed the ax from my mom's shaky hands, and, without saying one word, she walked into the yard to finish off the immortal duck.

My grandma introduced me to Chinese sausage when I was seven. I watched her boil two sticks of sausage in a roaring pot of water as I sat at the dining table. She sliced the dried meat into bite-sized pieces and placed them in front of me.

"What are these, Grandma?" I asked.

Her smile was warm. "Chinese sausage," she answered.

I popped one in my mouth, and soon my plate was empty, and my heart was full.

Chapter Nine

Genesis

"I'm really sorry, Janette. I wish I could stay and help longer," I say as I clock out.

"No worries. Do what you gotta do," Janette says while she totals up table six's lunch bill. "You saved my butt staying as long as you did. I really can't thank you enough."

"I just have to make sure I make it to Genesis' appointment on time. She needs a new earmold. Her old one is whistling really badly because it's too small," I explain.

"No need to explain," she responds kindly. "Hurry up and get goin'."

Janette is the most amazing boss I've ever had, but I guess I don't have much to compare it to since it was my first and only job, straight out of high school.

She owns a lovely cafe that was passed down to her from her mother, who had been the original owner. Janette's Cafe is slightly tucked away on the outskirts of the city, a hidden gem.

When I first started working at Janette's, I was blown away at the detailed decor. It looked like a wooden cabin. Every chair and table was carved out of dark mahogany wood. Each piece looked as if it was carefully handcrafted by a skilled woodworker. The cushions on the chairs and booths were a deep olive green, and there were endless amounts of paintings of the outdoors that lined the walls of the restaurant.

Janette was a kind, beautiful, middle-aged woman. Her blonde hair that was slightly peppered with gray was usually pulled back into a low ponytail. She was constantly working hard at the restaurant every day of the year, including holidays. Two of her older children were out of the house, staying on college campuses, but she still had one teenager at home. I always admired her work ethic and dedication toward the cafe and her family.

When Janette learned that I was pregnant with Genesis, she assured me she would make it her top priority to put my daughter first and work around whatever I needed. I think she also felt sorry for me because Liam had left me to raise Genesis on my own.

I remember when Liam had packed up his things and left me four months pregnant and alone in our apartment. I called out from work the following day. I was barely able to hold it together long enough to stay on the phone to tell Janette that I wouldn't be able to come in that morning for my shift.

"It's okay, Eva. We will make do. Take as much time as you need," she kindly told me over the phone.

I continued to call out from work five more times. I was a complete mess, and I don't think the pregnancy hormones were helping my situation either.

When I finally returned to work, Janette greeted me with a loving hug.

"Are you doing all right, Eva?" she asked.

"I'm okay," I said.

She could tell that I was lying. "You don't look like you are doing all right. You look like you are barely holding it together," she said bluntly. "Do you want to tell me what's going on?"

I nodded, and Janette took me aside to one of the tables in the dining room, away from most of the customers. She took the time to sit down and talk to me as I confided in her during the first half-hour of my shift. She held my hand to comfort me as I told her about Liam leaving the baby and me because he didn't want to ruin his life. Janette encouraged me to stay strong for my baby, who I carried in my womb.

Over the last ten years, Janette has become like a second mom to me. I have thought of her more as my "work mom," rather than my boss. When I came back to the cafe from my maternity leave, I explained to Janette how the audiologist had checked Genesis' hearing the day after she was born. I explained that the machine detecting her brain waves didn't show any activity when the audiologist had checked her left ear. Janette listened while I told her how upsetting it had been giving birth to Genesis without her father there.

I remember holding my mom's fragile arm in the delivery room. My mom stood tirelessly, helping the delivery nurse hold my other leg up while I pushed for three hours straight. I remember my mom's words encouraging me to push harder as each painful contraction presented itself. I remember my mom telling me she could see the baby's full head of hair as I exasperatedly pushed Genesis' head past my pelvic bone. I remember my mom cutting Genesis' umbilical cord after it was done feeding nutrients from my body into Genesis' body. I remember her telling me she had my eyes and a cute, wide Asian nose.

I remember thinking that my mom had done and said to me all the things Liam should have done in the delivery room. She was a replacement for Genesis' absent father. Liam should have been rooting me on while I gave birth to *his* daughter—the hardest thing I have ever done in my twenty-eight years of life. Liam should have been the one telling me that *his* daughter had my beautiful, brown eyes and long, thick eyelashes. Liam should have been the one wiping the sweat from my forehead as I held Genesis, swaddled in my arms. He should have been there beside me, admiring our blessing from God. Liam should have been by my side when Genesis failed her newborn screening test, but he wasn't.

I didn't think much of it when the audiologist set up her machine and placed the foam earbuds in Genesis' ears. I held my sleeping baby in my arms, thinking of how she was the most precious baby in the universe.

I named her Genesis because I knew this would be a new beginning for the both of us, and I was right. It was a new beginning.

"I'm not getting any readings in her left ear," the audiologist explained.

"What do you mean?" I asked, confused. "What does that mean?"

"Well, it could just be fluid blockage in the ear which wouldn't be anything to worry about." The doctor continued, "You will have to set up an appointment with the audiology department, so they can use a device to detect if there's any fluid."

A week after leaving the hospital, I took Genesis to the audiology department. I assumed the doctor would detect fluid in Genesis' ear, which could've been the cause of her temporary hearing loss. I thought the doctor would simply remove the blockage, and we would be on our way. I thought my perfect angel would be fine, but I was wrong.

"The ear looks free of fluid," Dr. Kearny replied. "Let's go ahead and take her into the room to run some tests and see what's going on."

I sat down in the recliner with Genesis cuddled up in my arms, wondering why they provided a recliner for us to relax in and not just a normal chair.

"As you already know, this test should take about an hour, give or take, depending on if she stays asleep," the doctor explained. "Once she falls asleep, I will put foam earbuds into her ears. This will allow me to feed sound into them. Then, I will place electrode pads on her forehead, so I can record her brain wave activity."

The audiologist dimmed the lights overhead. She temporarily left the room to give Genesis and me some privacy. I followed her instructions; I leaned back into the oversized recliner and began breastfeeding Genesis. I rocked her back and forth in the chair in hopes of her falling asleep. After about twenty minutes, Genesis finally closed her eyes, and Dr. Kearny entered the room. She proceeded with the test.

The next thirty minutes Dr. Kearny and I sat silently, only whispering when it was absolutely necessary, trying not to wake up Genesis. Endless clicking sounds produced by Dr. Kearny constantly pressing down on the mouse, were selfishly breaking the silence in the room.

Genesis woke up prematurely and was in an irritated mood. Sweet, but ear-piercing baby screams filled the air. Genesis' arm escaped my poor swaddle job, and she began to paw at her ear, attempting to remove the earbud. I gently bounced Genesis up and down in my arms, in hopes of soothing her.

"Shhh, it's okay, my sweet girl," I said to Genesis.

Dr. Kearny reached over and removed the earbuds from Genesis' ears and the electrode pads from her forehead.

"Okay, well I think that's all we are going to get from her today," Dr. Kearny said. "I got a decent amount of information, but let's try to schedule another session again next week."

By the end of that month and four stressful appointments later, Dr. Kearny suggested I get Genesis a hearing aid.

"You think she needs a hearing aid?" I asked sadly.

"I would highly recommend it," she explained. "The test results are telling me that Genesis has minor to moderate hearing loss in her left ear. Hopefully, getting her a hearing aid, will provide her with normal hearing. Luckily, her right ear is completely normal."

My heart began to crumble into a million pieces. How could she be saying this about my perfect baby girl?

"Unfortunately, a cochlear implant isn't an option. Her inner ear hearing loss is permanent, but you can still help her by providing her with a hearing aid."

Dr. Kearny handed me a couple folders. "Here is some information about support groups that can help you throughout the process. They can be really helpful," she assured me.

I felt overwhelmed and tried not to cry, hearing the truth. "Okay, thank you," I responded. My mind was in a haze.

"Also, here is a paper with the quotes for a few hearing aids that would fit Genesis' needs."

I looked down at the absurd prices on the paper. I placed my hand over my watery eyes. "I'm sorry," I said, and I quickly picked up the baby bag and rushed out of the room with Genesis in my arms. Genesis began crying along with me as I angrily punched the elevator button with my thumb, over and over again, impatiently waiting for the green arrow to light up.

Fried Rice

Genesis could sense the ache in my heart. She could sense the fear in my body and the hopelessness in my eyes.

What could have gone wrong? I started to blame myself. What did I eat while pregnant with Genesis? I never drank any alcohol. I vowed to stay away from preservatives and artificial food dyes. I knew there were studies stating they could cause chromosomal damage to the baby while she developed in the womb. I even ate more organic foods while pregnant. I tried to do everything to the "T." Chemicals maybe? I always tried to use vinegar to clean, even though it smelled like throw-up. I took my prenatal vitamins religiously even though the horse-sized pills made me gag every time. Maybe it was genetic? Maybe it was all in God's plan? Maybe it was my fault?

"Mom and I will pay for the hearing aid," my dad reassured me over the phone.

He knew Liam hadn't been keeping up with his child support payments, and our insurance wouldn't cover a hearing aid for Genesis. We would be paying out of pocket, $1,553.00, to be exact.

What would I do without the support of my parents? They were always there for me, emotionally and financially. Another blessing that came with being an

Asian American.

"Thank you," I said as I tried not to cry again.

"You need to work out your issues with Liam. Call him," my dad demanded.

"Dad, he doesn't—"

"It would be best for you and Genesis," he declared.

"Dad, he doesn't want anything to do with us," I confirmed.

Again, I think of Alice, secluded and alone.

Tears began to stream down my face. "Sorry, Dad, I... gotta go." My crying caused me to hyperventilate. "Thank you for offering to pay for—" I couldn't talk. My throat tightened as I continued to sob. My heart was hurting in multiple ways. I hung up.

The following morning, I found myself greeting my parents at Brandi's townhome. I was surprised to see them show up unannounced.

"What's going on?" I asked them.

"Just checking in to see how things are going," my mom said.

"I'm doing okay, and Genesis is doing okay," I said, unsuccessfully faking my bravery.

I turned to look at Genesis silently sleeping in her crib and then lunged at my mom, hugging her tiny body tightly.

"I don't know how I'm going to do this alone," I

said as my tears began to stain her blouse. She rubbed my back like she used to when I was five. She did this when I was younger to help me fall asleep. I was afraid the monsters under my bed were going to take me away to their labyrinth below.

I picked my head up off my mom's shoulder and wiped my nose on my wrist. My nose detected the smell of fried dumplings before my eyes spotted the takeout bags in my father's hands.

"You brought dim sum," I said.

My dad smiled. "We got you three orders of Ham Sui Gok."

"Your favorite," my mom added.

We sat down at the dining table and ate our comforting brunch together. I instantly felt better as I took a bite out of the sweet, crispy dumpling filled with pork. I was again reminded of the days when I was a little girl, grabbing at the bags of dim sum in my dad's hands as he returned home from work.

This was when I learned *food is a form of sympathy*.

Genesis and I had been through a lot together the first eleven months of her life. Many times, I had to pick myself up off the floor and encourage myself to stay strong for my daughter. Many times, I had to remind myself that giving birth to Genesis was the best day of my life. Many times, I had to tell myself I would not be defeated.

I pick up Genesis from my parents' house after rushing over from work.

"Sorry, I'm late. Someone on the night shift called out, and Janette asked me to stay a couple hours longer," I explain to my mom.

"No worries, Hunny," my mom assures me. "Genesis had fun with grandpa today."

Even though my parents didn't approve of Liam's and my nonexistent relationship, they had fallen in love with Genesis the moment she was born, and Genesis had fallen in love with her grandparents.

"Okay, we gotta go, sweetie, before we are late to your appointment," I say to Genesis. I take her from my mom's hip and grab her bag. "Say bye-bye to grandma and grandpa."

"Grampa, Grampa," Genesis says as she waves bye. My parents both take turns kissing Genesis on the top of her brown bobbed hairdo.

I thank my parents for babysitting while I rush out the door.

On the drive to see Genesis' doctor, I look down at my boobs. I'm still currently dressed in my light gray slacks and short-sleeved, white button-up shirt. I realize I had not pumped for over six hours, distracted by the overtime at the cafe. I rub the top of my right boob. "Oww." It's firm and bulging with breast milk.

I decide to try and breastfeed Genesis in the car before heading into the building for her appointment. She won't eat.

"Come on, baby, just a little," I try to coax her. No luck. "Grandma must have fed you right before I picked you up, didn't she my lovely, lady?" Genesis giggles loudly. Shit, okay. I button my shirt back up.

"Hi, appointment for Genesis?" the receptionist inquires.

"Yes, 3:30 appointment with Dr. Kearny," I respond. "We're supposed to pick up a new earmold."

"Okay, I will let her know you are here," Carol tells us. "It'll just be about five minutes or so."

"Thank you," I say as I take a seat in the waiting room. I pull out Genesis' favorite toy phone from her bag and hand it to her while I bounce her on my leg. I can feel the breast pads between my bra and boobs become saturated with uneaten milk. I also start to feel the saturation on my work slacks coming from the bottom of Genesis' baby butt.

"You POOP? Did you poop?" I yell frantically

while rapidly lifting her off my leg. "Oh, my gosh, you did, baby girl. Oh, no, no, no!"

I catch the receptionist's attention. She cringes. There's watery baby poop everywhere. It had blown out of Genesis' diaper, through her pink floral pants, and onto my leg. I could feel it on the skin of my thigh. "Ughhh! Okay, let's go, Genesis." I hold Genesis at the end of my arms and race to the family bathroom to clean us up.

"Okay, Genesis, I'm glad I had an extra pair of clothes in the bag for you. Maybe, I should start carrying an extra pair for me too," I say to her. I finish putting on her fresh, clean outfit and try to wipe off the baby poop from my pants while attempting to juggle her on my hip with one arm.

"Ugh! Baby girl! So stinky," I say while dry heaving. Genesis is such a happy baby, but sometimes I feel like she's laughing at me. There is still some residue leftover on my pants from the runny baby poop that won't completely wipe off. Lovely.

"Oh, no!" I say, looking into the bathroom mirror. I notice that my breast milk has leaked all the way through my pads, bra, undershirt, and onto my outer work shirt. "Nooo!" I howl. My hands ball up into tight fists.

"You okay in there?" a random lady asks while knocking on the door multiple times.

"FINNNE! I'm fine!" I respond. I'm annoyed because of my multi bodily fluid mishap. What a sweet lady, though. I yank my useless breast pads out and toss them angrily into the wastebasket. I look at Genesis in the mirror. She's still smiling and as happy as a clam. She is entertained by her reflection.

"All right. Everything is going to be fine," I say as I grab a handful of paper towels from the dispenser. I pat my shirt with the towels and try to collect the excess moisture. At least my boobs aren't writhing in as much pain anymore, I suppose.

"Okay, let's go Genesis." I look like crap and possibly like one of those college girls who had just participated in a wet T-shirt contest, minus the visibly hard nipples.

Dr. Kearny tries unsuccessfully to ignore my stained pants and the faint smell of baby poop coming from my leg. She unsuccessfully tries to avoid eye contact with my chest area.

"Okey-dokey, well, it looks like Genesis' new mold fits perfectly," the doctor says as she quickly steps away from us. After putting Genesis' sparkly, new mold in her ear, Dr. Kearny attempted to get as far away from me as possible, which wasn't very far considering we are in a pretty small room. I am aware the leftover poop on my leg reeks.

"Just remember to keep the old mold, in case you lose the new one or something happens to it," Dr. Kearny reminds me.

"Sure thing," I say.

As I follow Dr. Kearny out the door, I stumble. I'm carrying Genesis on my hip, and we become unsteady. I feel a hand under my arm, intentionally placed there for support. The man's hand helps Genesis and me regain our balance.

"Ahh! I'm so sorry!" I say apologetically. I hadn't watched where I was walking and had bumped into Dr. Grayson.

"I'm fine," he says, looking into my eyes, then at my wet boobs, and then at my poop stain. His eyes are gorgeous, to say the least. He reminds me of an older Prince Eric from the *Little Mermaid*. So dreamy. His long, flowy black hair is gently swept to the side. His light blue eyes are hypnotizing, and his sharp jawline encases his perfectly white smile.

"Are you girls okay?" he asks.

"Oh, heh, yeah we're good." I try to adjust Genesis in my arms, moving her more toward the front of my body in an attempt to try and hide the bodily fluids that cover my outfit. I feel the need to apologize again. "Sorry about that, Dr. Grayson."

He lightly chuckles. "No worries."

I already knew his name because of the nametag stitched onto the left side of his doctor's coat, but Dr. Kearny feels the need to formally introduce us. "Eva, this is Dr. Grayson. He just transferred to our hospital about a week ago."

"Nice to meet you, Eva," he says. I think he would've tried to shake my hand if I didn't look so disgusting. "Now, if you will excuse me." He heads into the room Dr. Kearny and I recently exited from.

"Go ahead and schedule a non-aided hearing test with Carol up front. Two or three weeks from now should be good," Dr. Kearny instructs as she leads me to the front desk.

"Does Tuesday, the 18th work okay for you?" Carol asks.

"Yes," I reply, wondering if I can schedule it with Dr. Grayson instead of Dr. Kearny. I wonder if he is single. I wonder if it would be inappropriate to date Genesis' doctor. Ah! What am I thinking?

Chapter Ten

Beach Day

"Look, Genesis, there's Auntie!" I say into my daughter's ear. I point at Brandi gliding along on the ocean's waves. "Auntie is having too much fun boogie boarding, isn't she?"

Genesis loudly taps her orange beach shovel against the rim of her sand pail. Thirty seconds after that, she throws down the shovel and scoops up a pile of sand with her hand. Before she can take a bite of sand, I gently grab her wrist.

"No, no, baby, that's yucky. You don't want to put that in your mouth. It won't taste good," I tell her as I remove the sand from her precious baby hand. Her skin is fair, just like mine. We are both lathered in a thick layer of sunscreen. Thankfully, I remembered to bring

Genesis' purple sun hat. She occasionally tugs at the bow at the bottom of her chin but isn't able to untie it. Genesis finds a silvery seashell and looks at it for a moment. She places it in the bucket and looks satisfied with herself.

Our beach day is faultless. The splendid sunshine resets my vitality. It's a perfect seventy-seven degrees in Coronado and not too windy. The dazzling, tropical scenery renews my vivacity. The sound of waves breaking on the shore clears my mind, and the salty air I breathe cleanses my soul.

"I told you it was a good idea to accompany me to the beach today," Brandi says, drying her wet hair with her beach towel.

"Yeah, I haven't seen the Hotel Del in years. I forgot how amazing the landscape is," I say as I stare at a couple of shredded guys skimboarding in front of us.

I begin to imagine one of the skimboarders leaving his board to wade in the waves of the sea as he spots me lying down on my back in the warm sand. I prop myself up onto my elbows, witnessing the dreamy, blue-eyed man making his way toward me. Palm trees are rustling behind him as he whips his long, wet blonde hair out of his face. I imagine the sexy hunk of a man running toward me in slow motion as dewy droplets of ocean water drip down his tanned skin. His body is sun-kissed from spending endless days at the beach. His chiseled eight-pack catches my eye as he comes nearer. "Hi, my name is Slatter," he says in his delicious man voice. Before I can introduce myself, he gets down on both of his knees and hovers over me. He kisses me wildly, and we begin to—

"You want me to watch Genesis, so you can go say hi to those ridiculously sexy dudes over there?" Brandi asks, half serious, interrupting my awesome daydream.

I return my focus to Genesis, smearing her hands in the sand. "Ha, ha," I reply. I playfully glare at Brandi.

I begin to imagine walking over to the hotties enjoying their day in the ocean. I begin to think about my post-baby stomach that now has a permanent kangaroo pouch. I begin to wince at the thought of my unwanted stretch marks that are slightly noticeable above my string bikini. I begin to think of my miniature-sized boobs that are deflated and uneven from attempting to end breastfeeding a few days ago. I feel self-conscious as I sit on the beach in the revealing bikini Brandi bought me last week.

"Look Eva, this one is so cute!" Brandi said. She held up a skimpy, black, string bikini. "You should try it on," she encouraged me.

"Mmm, no," I said. "Maybe two years ago. You

know before I had Genesis, and my body wasn't completely ruined." I shook my head and continued looking at the one-piece bathing suits on the rack. "I don't think I like any of these," I said quietly to myself. I felt discouraged about my post-baby body. "Okay, I think I'm about ready to go. Are you ready?" I asked Brandi.

"Wait, what? You didn't even try anything on," Brandi said, disappointed.

"Yeah, I think these aren't really my style. Maybe I will just order something online," I explained.

"But this is your favorite store." She started to swing her arms around like a madwoman. "Please, just try this one bikini on," she pleaded, holding the bikini directly in front of my face.

I shook my head. "No, my stomach looks disgusting after having Genesis." I walked out of the store, leaving Brandi behind. Then I looked over my shoulder to see if Brandi was following me, but instead, I saw her walk to the cashier's counter and purchase the bathing suit. She hurriedly stomped out of the store and caught up with me.

"You are beautiful and, more importantly, you gave birth to my beautiful niece. You should be proud of your strong body for enduring pregnancy and gifting the world with Genesis," Brandi said. She shoved the bag into the middle of my chest, forcing me to take the bikini.

I unwillingly took the bag and sighed, "Thank you. I love you." She gave me a side hug while we walked out of the mall and kissed my cheek.

"You are gorgeous, girl! Your body is amazing, and you better not forget it!" she said, screaming into my ear.

I take Genesis' hearing aid out and stick it in her baby bag. "Come on, pretty lady, your turn to go into the water," I tell her.

I stand up, not caring about the stomach I carried my magnificent child in for thirty-eight exciting but long weeks. I pick Genesis up off the sand, not concerned about how my breasts look from nourishing my marvelous daughter. I walk over to the ocean and set my gorgeous girl's toes in the warm, Pacific waters for the very first time.

I look at Brandi, sitting on her towel on the sand, and yell, "Take some pictures with my phone!" She pulls my phone out of the diaper bag and starts documenting Genesis' first day at the beach. I try to get Genesis to look toward the camera. "Come on, baby, look at Auntie," I encourage her.

The next thing I know, someone is yelling at me, "Watch out!"

Fried Rice

I wake up, confused. My eyes are blurry. I think I'm lying flat on my back, on the wet sand. As my eyes regain focus, I see Brandi holding Genesis.

Brandi is hovering over me, repeatedly asking me if I'm okay.

"I'm okay, I think. Is everything okay with Genesis? What happened?" I ask, worried.

"Yes, Genesis is okay. You blocked the skimboard from hitting her... with your head."

"I'm sorry! It was an accident. I didn't know she was so close," one of the ripped skimboarders says. "It was an accident. I swear."

Brandi shoos him away. "Eva, are you sure you are okay?"

"Yeah, I think I'm all right. Although my head feels like it got hit by a baseball bat," I say as I rub the side of my head. "So, I got hit in the head with a skimboard, and Genesis is all right?" I try to confirm as Brandi helps me sit upright.

"Yes, Eva. She's fine. Genesis is just crying a little bit because she's frightened you might've gotten hurt. Me too! You really scared us."

"Hi, are you ladies okay?" Some random guy bends down beside us to check if we need assistance. "I was just running by, and I saw what happened."

"Prince Eric? Is that you?" I ask as Brandi and the kind gentleman help me over to the dry sand, where our towels lay. "Are you taking me away to your castle?" My walk is unsteady.

"I think you might have a little bit of a concussion," Brandi says. She helps sit me down on the sand by our towels and hands Genesis over to the random guy helping us. "I better get Genesis over to your parents, so I can take care of you. I think you will be okay, though," she says and pauses to look me directly in the eyes. "Right? Eva, you're going be okay?" She starts to pack up our beach gear.

"Oh, my gosh. Hi, Dr. Grayson," I say as I realize he isn't some random man holding Genesis.

"Hi. I remember you from our office encounter the other day," he says. "It's nice to see you again, Eva." I feel my face turn bright red, but not from the sunrays. "You took quite a hit there."

"I guess I did, huh?" I say while trying to comb through my frizzy hair with my fingers.

"Oh, you guys know each other?" Brandi asks. She swings the baby bag over her shoulder, tucks our oversized beach towels under her arm, and begins to drag the boogie board in the sand toward the car. "Okay, good," she says. "Uh, Dr. Grayson, you go ahead and stay with Eva. Thank you for still holding Genesis, and I will be right back. I'm just going to put this in the car real quick. Do you think you can put your shirt and shorts on, Eva? If not, I will help you when I get back. Okay, be back in just a minute." Brandi slowly walks to the car. Whether it's because of the weight of her load or for other reasons, I'm not entirely sure.

"Thank you, Dr. Grayson, for helping us out," I say. "I think I might be okay now." I stand up to put my shirt and shorts on over my bikini. I can feel Dr. Grayson's eyes scan my half-naked body.

"Oh, you can call me Ken," he says as he shyly turns his head away. He looks at the seagulls, nibbling on someone's leftover scraps of food.

"Well, thank you, Ken. You have come to our rescue." I smile while looking into his charming blue eyes. I wonder if my feeble attempts at flirting are working. "How can I thank you?"

I try to take Genesis from his hands, but he refuses. "No, it's okay. I can walk you to the car." He shifts Genesis to the other side of his hip.

"Oh, okay, thank you. I really appreciate it. Maybe I could cook you dinner one night to thank you for helping us and for interrupting your run." My eyes start to scan his fit body. He's dressed in jogging shorts and running shoes. His chest reminds me of the two skimboarders' irresistible upper bodies. We definitely picked the right day for a beach day. That's for sure!

"You don't have to do that," he explains.

"No, I want to. I really do. Please, let me cook you dinner. I mean, unless you think it's unprofessional… or something? I don't want to get you in trouble—"

"No, no, I won't get into any trouble at work. Uh, yeah, you know what? I would love for you to cook me dinner. It's a date. Wait, is it a date?"

I laugh. "Yeah, it can be a date. My place… well, Brandi's place. Genesis and I live with Brandi at her townhome," I explain. "Would you like to come over tomorrow night? Does 5:30 sound good? I can drop Genesis off at my parents for a couple hours if you want."

"Absolutely!" he says. We exchange numbers after he buckles Genesis into her car seat. "Bye-bye, Genesis! I will see you soon." She smiles at Ken from inside the car.

"Thanks, Dr. Grayson," Brandi says as she closes the trunk. "All set."

"Bye, ladies. I will see you tomorrow, Eva. Text me the address," he orders. He turns back toward the beach and continues his run. I think of how fate might have brought us together for a good reason.

"He's a hottie," Brandi says as we get into the car. "You gonna thank him tomorrow, aren't ya? Huh, Eva?

Are you?" Her mind is in the gutter. She pushes her tongue against the inside of her cheek and raises her loose fist to her mouth like she's sucking on a man's molten member.

I shove the side of Brandi's shoulder with the side of my fist, and I give her a sinister glare. "Classy, real classy, Brandi," I say. We both laugh.

"You seem fine. I think I can take both of you home with me. I will call out of work tonight to keep an eye on you, just as a precaution, and help you take care of Genesis."

"What would I do without you, Brandi? You are the greatest," I say to my best friend, my sister.

"Oh, so, I know you got hit in the head pretty hard with the skimboard and all..." Brandi mentions. "But why did you call Dr. Grayson Prince Eric?"

"Oh, my gosh. I called him Prince Eric? Oh, no. I can't believe I did that, Brandi. Brandi, why did I do that?" I say, panicking.

"He does look like a handsome Prince Eric from *The Little Mermaid*," she says, agreeing with my concussed thoughts. We smile at one another.

"I know, right?"

Chapter Eleven

Date with Dr. Ken

"You look so fabulous, lady!" I say to Brandi as she spins around in her flowing Hawaiian dress.

"Thank you," she replies. "I'm off to spend the night at a hotel on Shelter Island with Max. He paid for a room and wants to treat me to a *special* date night. I'm so excited!"

"Oh, fancy!" I exclaim.

"I should be back sometime tomorrow afternoon," she says, slipping on her sandals. "And I better not come home to you and Dr. Grayson snuggled up on your couch bed after a long night of hot, horny sex! Not until the second date," Brandi jokes. Or, at least, I think she's joking.

She grabs her overnight bag and points her finger at me, "You better save me some of those egg rolls you are making. Oh! And some of that bomb-ass jook too!"

I laugh at her. "I will. I made extra," I assure her as she walks out the door.

As I stir the jook in the oversized pot, it reminds me of my great-grandpa on my mom's side coming over to the States from China. He came to the U.S. in search of better opportunities. He wanted to give himself and his family in China a better life. My great-grandpa ended up marrying a Cajun woman and started a second family in the States. It's crazy to think about him having two families that were an ocean apart.

I imagine my great-grandpa tirelessly straining his back, working on the railroads, sometime in the early 1900s. I imagine him sitting down for dinner, after a long day's work and eating jook, which at the time was a "poor man's" dish. I imagine his body's strength being restored by the nourishment from the poultry carcasses. I imagined him being comforted by the warmth of the porridge.

I finish frying up the egg rolls and set a handful of them onto a plate. I place them next to the glass bowl of sweet and sour sauce that is on the dining table. The egg rolls and sauce are both made from scratch.

I quickly change out of my scrubby clothes and put on my nicest dress. It really isn't that nice at all; it's just a casual, short-sleeved dress, but I think it will do. I let my hair down, pulling the band from my head, which releases my messy bun. I put a light coat of makeup on, and I am good to go for my date with Ken.

Sasuke runs to the door and starts viciously barking, notifying me that someone is coming up the front walkway. I open the door and see Ken standing in front of me with a bright smile on his face.

"Hi, Eva. I brought these for you," Ken says and hands me a bouquet of Gerber daisies. "I wasn't sure what your favorite flower is."

"I love them. They are perfect," I say.

Red tulips are my favorite, but the orange daisies are beautiful. I pull out a ceramic vase from one of the kitchen cabinets and place the flowers in water. Sasuke is following Ken around as he walks through the living room, still barking at him.

"Sasuke! No more barking!" I tell Brandi's wiener dog, but Sasuke doesn't listen. He begins to aggressively nip at Ken's nice shoes. I run over toward Ken, pick up Sasuke, and put him outside. "I'm sorry about that. He's usually a little nervous around strangers. Their breed is really loyal to family and close friends. He's just trying to protect us," I try to explain.

"It's quite all right," he tells me, but he bends down to try and rub the scratches off his dress shoes caused by

Sasuke's teeth. He looks slightly annoyed. "You look nice this evening," Ken says.

I'm glad I had changed my outfit because Ken looks really handsome. He is dressed in a long-sleeved, buttoned-up shirt, and he's wearing black slacks with his now ruined dress shoes.

"Thank you. So do you." I smile.

Ken eyes the egg rolls on the dining table. "Oh! I love egg rolls," he says excitedly.

"My family's recipe," I say proudly. "I hope you like them."

He eagerly sits down, and I hear a loud crunch as Ken bites into his egg roll. "Oh, wow, these *are* really good." His eyes light up as he takes another bite. "Usually, I just buy the mediocre, frozen ones at the grocery store, but these are a hundred times better," he says as he finishes off the crunchy egg roll. "The sauce is fantastic too."

"I'm glad you like it," I say, happily. "I also made some jook." I spoon the porridge out of the large pot and into my Chinese soup bowls.

"I'm not sure I'm familiar with, uh, jook," he says while reaching for a second egg roll.

"It's basically a porridge. Some people call it congee. It's one of my favorite comfort foods." I carefully walk to the table with the bowls of jook in my hands.

"Oh, okay. It looks good," Ken says, unsure of himself.

"I know it doesn't look super appetizing, but I promise, it tastes great."

I walk back to the kitchen and grab Chinese soup spoons from the drawer. When I had first moved in with Brandi, my mom had given me a couple of her nice ceramic spoons to keep at the townhome. "Here," I hand Ken the spoon. "For whatever reason, it always tastes better when you eat it with one of these," I say sarcastically.

"Thank you," he says.

"No, really… thank you for helping take care of Genesis and me at the beach. It would've been a lot more stressful for Brandi if you weren't there to help. Oh! I almost forgot. Hold on."

I run over to the kitchen and pull out the soy sauce, sriracha sauce, and a small bowl of chopped green onions. I juggle all the toppings in my hands as I walk back to the table.

"Okay, here. You can add some or all of these on top of the jook," I instruct him.

"Oh, okay. What's sriracha?" he asks and puts a little bit of soy sauce and green onions in his bowl. "I don't eat much Asian food as you can probably tell."

"It's kind of hot. It's made from chili peppers," I

explain.

"I'll give it a shot," he says.

We mix up our toppings in our jook, and we simultaneously take a bite of the porridge.

"Oh, wow, Eva. This is really delicious. The texture is a little different, but I like it."

"Yeah, it kind of feels like you are eating mushy brains if you close your eyes," I say, laughing at my joke, but Ken doesn't join in, which makes me feel a little uncomfortable. "Well, uh, that makes me really happy to hear that you like it." I smile.

"So, is this another one of your family's secret recipes?"

"I don't know about a *secret* recipe, but yes, my mom learned it from my grandma, who learned it from her mom, etcetera, etcetera. We usually eat it after making a turkey, so the bones and extra meat don't go to waste, like after Thanksgiving and whatnot. Although, I used chicken in this one. Sometimes, Genesis likes it when I cut up roasted chicken for her as a snack," I explain.

He ignores my comment about Genesis. "Did this take you a long time to cook?" he asks, curiously.

"Not too long," I say, modestly.

Realistically, it had taken me a solid three hours, if not longer, to complete everything from start to finish. "It was fairly easy. I only had to chop up a few ingredients for the egg rolls. It's just time-consuming to roll all of them up. I also had to make extra for Brandi. I just threw a few ingredients into a pot to make the jook," I explain, simplifying my cooking process.

"Well, this is spectacular," he says as he cleans his bowl. "You have officially thanked me." He helps himself to another egg roll and dunks it into the sauce.

This was when I realized *food is a form of gratitude.*

"Which one did you like best?" I ask him. "The egg rolls or the jook?"

He takes a minute to think, "Ah, it's a hard one, but I think I would have to go with the jook."

"I can get you some more," I say and scoop up his empty bowl.

Ken rubs his stomach. "Okay, but just one more bowl. My pants are starting to get too tight from all the delicious food you are feeding me."

"Of course," I reply. Not that I was really asking.

"My mother went to culinary school," Ken mentions. "I think she would've loved the meal you cooked for us."

"You think so? Thank you for saying that," I reply. "Culinary school? That sounds like a lot of fun."

"Yes, she thoroughly enjoyed it. She interned at a French fine dining restaurant and eventually gained a permanent position as a cook. Within months, she had worked her way up to sous-chef." He is clearly impressed at his mom's accomplishments.

"That's so awesome. So, what restaurant is she working at now? The same one she interned at?"

Ken pauses for almost an entire minute. He looks like he's lost in a daydream. I start to ask my question again, thinking he might've not heard me the first time, "So, what restaurant does she work—"

"I apologize. She doesn't work at a restaurant any longer. My mother became pregnant shortly after marrying my father. My father was able to financially support the three of us on his own, so there was really no need for her to continue working. My younger sister, Emily, came along just a few years after my mom had me. My mother told me that staying home with her children was the best decision she had ever made."

"I bet you grew up with some amazing meals too?" We smile at each other.

"Uh, yeah. I definitely did," he explains. "My mother would always try to get Emily to join her in the kitchen. She wanted to teach Emily different cooking techniques, but it wasn't really my sister's thing. I really loved it, though. I learned a great deal about cooking from my mother, but I would have to say my favorite part was making desserts with her."

"Oh, no. I didn't plan for dessert! You just reminded me," I say, bummed I hadn't remembered. "I'm sorry. I—"

"No need to apologize. I am extremely full. I don't think I would've had room for dessert."

"Okay," I say, feeling more at ease. "Can I at least pack you up a to-go box? There's a lot of leftovers."

"I would love to take some home," he says. "I would *also* love to see you again in the near future."

I slide the containers of leftovers into the fridge.

"Oh, you would?" I smile with excitement. I notice the tallies on the whiteboard and laugh in its face. I happily take it off the fridge so it can hibernate in Brandi's junk drawer. I turn around and lean back onto the kitchen counter. "I would really, uh, love that too," I say, nodding my head. I seductively bite my lower lip. I think I might look sexy leaning against the kitchen counter… maybe? I twirl a strand of my hair for more enticement.

"Come sit down with me," he orders. I sit next to him. "You worked so hard making this lovely dinner for me today," he says as he grabs the top of my hand. "You should sit down and relax a little."

Now, I am, *for sure*, blushing and wondering if *I'm* about to get rewarded for making him a wonderful dinner. Or maybe I should still be rewarding him? I think back to Brandi's skanky humor in the car.

He catches me by surprise and gently kisses my cheek. I can't remember what I was thinking about a second ago. I giggle like a little schoolgirl who is flirting with one of her classmates.

"So, what do you say about me cooking you a nice dinner next weekend?" he asks. "At my place?"

"Yeah, that sounds amazing," I say.

"Terrific! Well, it's getting late. I should probably head on home." I hand Ken his leftovers and patiently wait for a goodbye kiss. "Thank you again for dinner, Eva," he says, and he softly kisses my cheek... again. "You are so fantastic. I can't wait to see you next weekend."

Ken walks out the door and looks back at me from over his shoulder. He waves bye as I watch him go. I am alone and yearning for more.

Chapter Twelve

Kona Kai

Brandi returns from her date night with Max, and she storms into the kitchen as I make Genesis' lunch. "Oh, my gosh!" she says and squeals excitedly. "Guess what happened last night?" I notice she's hiding her hands behind her back.

"Umm, did you…" I think for a moment while she does a happy dance with her legs. It kind of looks like the "pee-pee" dance kids do when they are about to have an accident. I gasp, and my eyes widen. "DID YOU GET ENGAGED?" I pull her hand from behind her back and into plain sight.

She has the biggest smile strewn across her face. I look down at her hand and see a beautiful gold band accompanied by a sizable diamond. It looks dazzling. "Oh, my gosh! You did! You did get engaged!"

"Yes!" she yells. We start jumping up and down like

two little girls who are excitedly playing on a trampoline. Once we exhaust our physical excitement, Brandi continues, "He proposed to me during dinner. It was perfect! The restaurant overlooked hundreds of boats on the marina. He confessed his undeniable love for me and proposed as the sun started to set. It was the best night I've ever had!"

I look Brandi in her eyes. Both of us are laughing while tears stream down our faces. "I am so happy for you, Brandi. Max truly is a lucky man." I tightly embrace her in my arms. "I love you so much. Congrats, girl."

"I love you too, Eva!"

"Max is such a great guy. I *cannot* wait for him to officially be a part of our family," I say.

As we wipe away our happy tears, Brandi says, "Oh, I need to call my mom and dad!" She pulls out her phone and heads to her room to share the good news.

I look at Genesis in her highchair. She is giggling and patiently waiting for her lunch, which is uncommon. Usually, she is demanding her food by screaming or slapping the top of the highchair tray. "You are being so good, my little princess. Did you hear? Auntie is getting married!" I walk over to her and kiss her on her forehead. Genesis smiles and says, "Mama, Mama." She is encouraging me to feed her.

I place diced pieces of mozzarella cheese and

strawberries onto her tray. She quickly digs in. "Well, it looks like you are enjoying your wine tasting platter, aren't ya, baby girl?" Genesis nods her head in approval.

Brandi looks like she is walking on clouds as she returns to the kitchen. She kisses Genesis on her strawberry-stained cheek and sits down next to my daughter at the kitchen table.

"Did you already eat lunch?" I ask Brandi.

"No, not yet," she answers.

"I'll heat you up a couple egg rolls I made yesterday."

"Oh, sorry, Eva. I didn't ask you about your date last night," Brandi apologizes.

"You don't need to apologize! I'd really rather talk more about your wedding plans anyway!" I say excitedly.

"Oh, it didn't go all that great with Ken last night?" she asks, unsure.

"Actually, it went really well," I tell her. "He loved my dinner. We talked about our family and cooking the majority of the night."

"Annnnnd?"

"And what?" I ask.

"And did you guys bone on the couch bed?" she says, unable to hold back her laughter.

"Don't say bone, Brandi!"

"Okay." She rolls her eyes. "Did you guys make

sweet, *sweet* love together?"

I shake my head while chuckling to myself. "No, Brandi, we did not. He held my hand and kissed me on the cheek. That was it."

She gasps and smiles at me. "He brought you those flowers, didn't he?"

"Yeah. He's a super sweet guy. I have plans to go over to his place next weekend."

Brandi abruptly stands up. "You mean a second date at Dr. Grayson's house?" She doesn't wait for a response. "Bow chicka wow wow," she sings as she does a weird, pervy dance with her hips.

"Oh, my gosh, Brandi!" I exclaim.

Genesis claps her hands. "Auntie, Auntie!" she says.

"Don't encourage her, Genesis!" I yell at my daughter.

"Oh, come on! Genesis thinks I'm a good dancer!" Brandi says.

I roll my eyes. "Anyway, so tell me more about your plans for the wedding."

"Well, we haven't talked about it too much, but we definitely want it to be a long engagement. We don't want to have to stress too much about rushing to plan a wedding," she says.

"Like how long of an engagement? I don't want to wait my whole life for this wedding," I say.

"Oh, probably about a year or so. Not too long," she explains. "We want to get married on the beach or somewhere overlooking the ocean." I could've guessed that. "It'll be sometime in the middle of next summer," she assures me. "Of course, I want you to be my maid of honor. I'm not even asking you because you don't have a choice." She smiles.

I hug her again. "You are making me cry way too much today!" I say to her.

"And I figure about a year from now, Genesis will be able to walk pretty well. So, she can be my flower—"

I embrace her tightly for the third time this afternoon, and I don't care if I am suffocating her with my excitement.

Chapter Thirteen

Two Dresses

As I return home from the cafe, I notice a box sitting in front of the doorstep. "A package?" I pick up the box and see that it's addressed to me.

"Hey, Eva. You have a good day at work?" Brandi asks. She is sitting on the couch eating a bowl of chow mein I made the other day.

"Yeah," I answer, distracted by the package.

"What's that?" Brandi asks.

"I'm not sure." I sit down next to Brandi, anxious to see who the package is from.

"Where's Genesis?" Brandi asks. "I thought you were supposed to pick her up at your parents' after you got off from work?"

"Oh, my mom wanted a little more time with her,

so, they told me they would drop her off in a couple hours," I say. I tear the tape off the package and open the flaps.

"Oh, you ordered a dress?" Brandi asks. I ignore her as I pull out a second dress. "Oh, you ordered *two* dresses?"

I shake my head. "No."

"There's a letter," Brandi says. She picks up the paper that had fallen on the couch. Brandi and I read the letter together.

Dear Eva,

I ordered you these dresses. I hope they are to your liking. I know you will look gorgeous in either one. I was thinking you could wear one this weekend and the other one on our next date.

- Ken AKA Prince Eric

"Prince Eric?" Brandi cackles. "You sure you guys didn't bone last weekend?"

I stare at Brandi, horrified. I hold up one of the dresses and then the other. "I don't want to wear either of these dresses."

"The dresses are beautiful," Brandi says. "You are going to look so hot! Try them on now!" she demands.

I stall and continue to look at the dresses. I start to

reread the letter Ken wrote me.

"Hurry, before I have to go to work! You're going to have to wear one tomorrow anyway," she says while shoving me off the couch.

I grumble, "Okay, fine!"

Brandi sets down her half-eaten bowl of noodles on the sofa and repeatedly claps her hands, excited for an extremely short and super lame fashion show.

"I guess I'll try this long-sleeved one on first," I say to myself as I undress in the bathroom.

The first dress is a dark purple, velvety cocktail dress. "What the hell?" I look at myself in the mirror. "Is he gonna make me a drink tomorrow?" I shrug at my reflection. "I guess I'd be down."

I walk out into the living room. "Ta-da." I look at my boobs hanging out of the dress.

"I like it! Your boobs look nice," Brandi says, one hundred percent serious.

The V-neck drops all the way past my sternum. "Okay, if you say so," I say, feeling like a prostitute. "You sure I shouldn't be standing on a street corner somewhere in this dress? My saggy boobs are popping out everywhere, and it's barely covering my butt," I say, dissatisfied.

Brandi laughs. "You are ridiculous! Your boobs aren't saggy. You look good, girl. I really like the ruching on the side of the dress. Dr. Grayson has good taste." She flings the back of her hand at me, impatiently shooing me back into the bathroom to try on the second dress. "Okay, next!" Brandi orders.

I walk back into the bathroom, tugging at the hem of the dress, and try to see how long I can make it, but my boobs just end up hanging out more. "I guess I could try to wear my push-up bra," I say to myself. I haven't worn one in over a year. I wonder if the old one I have still fits. Then I can really make some money standing on a street corner somewhere, like a *high-end* prostitute.

"As if the first one wasn't bad enough," I say as I continue my fashion show.

Brandi's eyes light up. "Ooh, I like this one," she says, and she scoots to the edge of the couch to get a closer look.

The second dress I try on is long, black, and really revealing. It has spaghetti straps that crisscross in the back with a huge, plunging neckline in the front. "I guess I can't wear a bra with this one?" I say, highly disappointed. "At least it's long, I suppose. I feel like you can almost see the top of my butt crack." I turn around to show Brandi the back of the dress.

"Your butt crack isn't showing." She laughs. "And as for the bra issue, I can let you have some of my pasties to hide your rock-hard nipples," Brandi offers.

"Or you can go bra-less, and Dr. Grayson can have dinner and a *show*." Brandi slaps her thigh. She's amused by her jokes. "No, but really, I do like the tulle fabric."

"It looks like a long tutu," I tell her. "I'm, straight up, a ballerina."

"So, which one are you going to wear tomorrow?" Brandi asks. "You have to pick one."

"I'm not sure. I haven't worn something this revealing since our high school prom," I tell her. My prom date, Jerry, had grossly grabbed my chest in the front seat of his Neon. That night I took a vow to forever wear outfits with a higher neckline.

"Ah, yeah. I remember you telling me about that," Brandi says. "Didn't you slap Jerry on the face and end up walking home by yourself?"

"Yeah, I kind of regret that. Not the whole slapping Jerry thing, but my shoes gave me the worst blisters. I walked almost a whole mile in heels before I sat down on the curb and called my dad to pick me up."

"I wish I could've seen the look on Jerry's face!" Brandi says.

"Anyway, which dress do you think I should wear?" I ask.

"You look amazing in both dresses. I don't think it really matters. You're going to have to wear the other one on your third date with Ken anyway!" She starts to laugh at my uncertainty. Yeah, she's definitely laughing at me again.

"I'll just decide tomorrow," I say.

"Okay, I will leave a couple pasties out on the top of my dresser in case you need them." She smirks.

Chapter Fourteen

Dr. Ken's Palace

"Am I at the wrong house?" I say to myself as I drive around a ginormous, concrete fountain. I put my car in park and take out my phone. I look at Ken's text—*5535 Inspirationals St., La Jolla.* The address on the house matches. I pull my car back around, staring at the ornate fountain again, and park next to the flashy yellow Porsche.

"Oh, my gosh!" I say to myself. I stand in the driveway wearing the ebony dress Ken had bought for me, pasties and all. "What the heck?" I pull my phone out of my sequined clutch and take a picture to send to Brandi. "Brandi's going to crap her pants when she sees this."

I tilt my head up in awe of the ridiculously large mansion in front of me. It had to be at least five times as big, if not bigger than Brandi's townhome. Balconies lined the bedrooms on the second story. The pearly white mansion is surrounded by perfectly groomed bushes and palm trees, and there are elegant rose bushes lining the walkway.

"Hi, Eva. I thought I heard you pull into the driveway," Ken says, catching me off guard.

"Hi, uh—" I stutter as I continue to stare at his insane mansion.

He gently hugs me. "I knew that dress would look stunning on you," Ken says. He is wearing a slick black suit. "Come on, let's go ahead and get you inside."

"So, this is your palace—place?" I stutter, quickly correcting myself. There's no way someone can afford something this glamorous, especially on an audiologist's salary.

"Yes. This is my place. Well, mine and my sister's," he answers.

"Oh, Emily? Can I meet her?" I ask, still shocked.

"I'm sure she would love to meet you, but she's actually away at college at the moment. She's staying on the school campus while she studies to become a lawyer. The college is in Los Angeles. Luckily, she's not too far away."

"Oh, uh, okay," I say as my head tilts back again. I stare at the crystal chandelier that hangs a good fifty feet above my head. "Oh, Los Angeles? Yeah, that's where my parent's met before they moved to San Diego. My dad ate at the restaurant my mom worked at," I awkwardly ramble on.

"You will have to tell me more about that during dinner," Ken says.

I notice the Grayson's sizable family portrait above the stone fireplace. "Your parents and Emily are beautiful. That's a wonderful family portrait."

Ken doesn't respond to my compliments. He sets his hand on my back and leads me through the mansion toward the backyard. "Oh, my goodness! When can I cook in your kitchen?" I say, half-jokingly. The kitchen is as big as Brandi's townhome. Every inch is immaculate. There's an eight-burner stove and two ovens stacked on top of one another. All the appliances are stainless steel, and the countertops are made of granite.

Ken chuckles. "I'd be more than happy to give you a tour after dinner if you'd like."

Heck yes, I want a tour! I think to myself. "That would be amazing," I say calmly, trying to suppress my excitement.

"All right, but I don't want our food to get cold," Ken says and escorts me to his backyard.

The backyard is just as amazing as his house, complete with an infinity pool—tall palm trees by the Jacuzzi tub sway in the coastal breeze. I think I see a tennis court in the distance. It's kind of dark, so I can't quite make it out.

"Wow, this is amazing, Ken," I say as I look at the lights strung above our intimate dinner table.

He pulls out my chair for me. "I made you some surf and turf. One of my favorite meals I loved making with my mom."

The plate looked like something you would order from an expensive restaurant. "You made this?" I say, surprised.

"My mom was an excellent teacher," he confirmed while shooting me a modest smile.

There was a decent-sized filet sitting next to a fancy-looking lobster tail. Large pieces of asparagus were placed alongside the steak, which sat under a small pile of mashed potatoes. There is some type of yellowish sauce drizzled over the vegetables.

"This looks way too good to eat," I say, and I quickly place the cloth napkin on my lap. "The mashed potatoes look so creamy."

"Oh, it's actually a turnip puree," Ken corrects me. "But, yes, it's similar to mashed potatoes. It definitely looks like… mashed potatoes." I think he's trying to make sure I don't feel bad for incorrectly labeling his food.

"Is this some type of hollandaise sauce?" I ask,

pointing at my plate. "The same sauce that usually comes on eggs Benedict?"

"I'm impressed," Ken says.

"I've eaten a lot of Benedicts back in my day, and it's also on the menu at the cafe I work at," I tell him. I take a bite of the filet. "Oh, my gosh!" I'm entranced by the perfect steak I am currently eating. "It's melting in my mouth." I'm talking with a mouthful of food, but I don't care and, thankfully, neither does Ken.

"I'm glad you are enjoying it, Eva," he says. "I'm not sure it compares to your family's sacred dishes, though. You can really taste the love of multiple generations in your cooking. I don't think this meal comes even remotely close to the meal you cooked me last weekend."

"You are so sweet. Thank you, but I don't believe you." I laugh and shove another piece of steak into my drooling mouth. "So, tell me, Ken, how do you and your sister afford a place like this?" Ken stops eating, sets his fork down, swallows deeply, and stares at his plate. "What's wrong?" I ask. "Did I say something?"

He stalls and dabs his mouth with his napkin.

"I knew I would have to tell you eventually, especially if I invited you over." I pause from eating as well and wait patiently. Ken looks dejected.

"It's okay. You can talk to me," I say. "But, if you

107

don't want to tell me something, you don't have to."

"No, I want to tell you," he says and deeply inhales. "My parents passed away in a car crash about a year ago."

"Oh, my gosh. I'm so sorry to hear that, Ken," I say, empathetically. "I mean, I couldn't imagine living without my parents."

Ken is silent and continues to stare blankly at his plate. I stand up, lean over the table, and place my hand under his chin. I smile, and his eyes meet mine. I kiss him on the lips and temporarily erase his sorrows. "I'm here if you need to talk."

"Thank you, Eva," Ken says. I sit back down, and we finish eating our dinner.

"I'm sure your mom and dad would've been so proud of you," I say to him. "Your mom would've been impressed by this perfect plate of food you cooked for us, and I'm sure your dad would be proud of your career. You get to help so many people."

"Yes, I'd like to think that too," he says. "Although, I think my dad was hoping I would follow in his footsteps and have a career in sports."

I'm happy that he is able to open up to me. "What did your dad do for a living?"

"My father played major league baseball," he explains. "When my mother and father passed, they left my sister and me everything."

"They sound like they were good parents," I say, confidently. "Tell me more about your dad. I bet you had the best time playing catch with him in your backyard."

"They were terrific parents," he says. "My father tried to get me into baseball as well as a bunch of other sports, but I'm really not all that coordinated. At least, not coordinated enough to make a career out of it. The pressure to become a professional in sports was overwhelming at times. Although, I knew he wanted the best for me."

"So, then, what made you decide to become an audiologist?" I ask. I wanted to ask why he was still even working, living in this huge mansion of his.

He sighs. "When my mother gave birth to my sister, it was really hard for my family." I placed my hand on the top of his, gently stroking his hand with my fingertips, urging him to continue. "Emily was born with moderate to profound hearing loss in both of her ears," he says. "What am I saying? You probably know how it is with Genesis' hearing loss and all," Ken reminds me.

I nod my head. "Yeah, it was tough, but mostly because I had to do it on my own. I mean, I had Brandi and my parents to help me, and I'm so thankful for that, but it just wasn't the—"

"It wasn't the same?" Ken finishes my sentence.

"Yeah, it just wasn't the same," I say. "Genesis not having a dad and me not having a husband or even a boyfriend to help raise a newborn... It's been pretty hard, but I guess it can always be worse, right?" I instantly regret saying that last part, thinking back to his parents' accident. "But, wow, I can't imagine Genesis having hearing loss in both ears."

"Yes, my sister is one of the lucky ones, though. Her hearing is pretty much normal now due to her successful surgery and cochlear implants." He smiles. "And what do you know? She's currently studying away, almost ready to become a lawyer."

"So, why are you still working?" I ask. "Do you really even need to keep working?" Was that rude of me to ask? Oh, well. I really want to know.

"I love my job. I don't want to be stuck at home all day. It helps keep me from feeling sorry for myself. If I stayed at home all day, I wouldn't be able to stop thinking about my parents' accident," he explains.

I feel terrible for Ken and try to lighten the mood. "You could just spend your days on the beach all day, every day. Who knows, maybe you would come across another damsel in distress." I quietly laugh. I begin to imagine him shirtless, running toward me on the beach in slow motion.

"I could." He chuckles. "Also, I often think about how my sister would come home crying before she received her surgery. Kids would constantly bully her at school because of her hearing aids."

"Kids can be so cruel," I say. "Well, it really is amazing to think of all the lives you've helped change."

"Yes, thank you, Eva. I just want to continue to help kids succeed in life by giving them a better chance," he says while picking up our empty plates.

"You are truly a great doctor," I tell him.

"I'm going to go get our dessert now." He grins at me, exposing his perfect smile. "I'll be right back. Don't leave."

I laugh to myself. Who in their right mind would voluntarily leave a place like this? I feel like I'm at a five-star resort. As I wait for Ken to come back with our desserts, I start to think of a conversation I had with my mom when I started dating Liam. Liam's family had money, but they weren't the same kind of wealthy Ken is.

"You know, life is a lot easier when you marry someone with money," my mom told me.

"Are you saying I should marry Liam for his family's money?" I asked.

"No, I'm just saying"—my mom tried to explain

herself—"that life is a lot less stressful when you don't have to worry about paying your bills. Life is much easier when you aren't living paycheck to paycheck."

"Okay, so you are saying I should be a gold digger and marry for money and not for love?" I became irate. I felt like my mom was trying to dictate my future.

"Eva, that's not what I'm saying at all."

Until my mom's grandparents had passed away, she remained pretty poor. The passing of my great-grandparents led my grandma and grandpa to sell the farm and move to Los Angeles to start up a Chinese restaurant. The menu consisted of many of our family dishes that have been passed down from multiple generations. The restaurant became pretty successful with my mom as the main cook.

The restaurant is also where she met my dad. He often ate lunch at my mom's family restaurant. Whenever my dad sat down at his normal table, my mom always found some excuse to say hi to him. Over the course of a couple years, they fell in love.

Shortly after they got married, my parents moved to San Diego. My parents struggled financially for the first few years of their marriage until my dad was offered a good paying desk job. Finally, they weren't living paycheck to paycheck. It wasn't until he was promoted to Business Operations Manager that they were able to

Fried Rice

buy a house of their own.

I know my mom didn't want to see me struggle like she and my dad did at the beginning of their marriage. She wanted me to have an easier life than she had.

"Here we go," Ken says as he sets the dessert in front of me.

"I love crème brûlée," I say. I pick up my spoon and crack the sugary shell. "Mmm, so good!" My eyes roll to the back of my head.

Ken chuckles at my exaggeration. "Eva, I'm glad you bumped into me at the office, and I'm thankful you got knocked unconscious on the beach while I was running."

I laugh. "Me... too?"

"I want to take you out to a really nice restaurant next weekend if you would let me?"

"Okay," I say, smiling as I scrape the bottom of the ramekin. "I will let you take me on another fancy, shmanshy date. I mean, I already have the outfit ready to go."

"I really do think my mom would have been proud of the dinner I made us tonight," he says. I can tell he's thinking about her again. Missing her in Heaven.

This was when I learned *food is a form of remembrance.*

*****

"Okay, what about that tour?" I ask him, anxiously. "I mean, I've been pretty patient, wouldn't you say?"

"Yes, you sure have, Eva," he says and walks around the table to pull my chair out.

After our tour is complete, Ken walks me to my car. I'm kind of bummed that he didn't throw me down on one of the beds and make sweet, amazing love to me until the sun came up. Any one of the six beds would've sufficed. Six times he got my hopes up, and six times I was let down. There's always next time, right?

"Your parents' house really is… I can't think of the right word! It's really beautiful. They had great taste."

"Thank you, Eva. You really are one in a billion," he says as he holds my hips. My arms are draped over the top of his shoulders. He gently kisses me on my impatient lips. I don't want this night to end, but eventually, he pulls always. I sit down in the driver's seat of my car. He closes my door and walks backward toward the mansion, waving at me. I drive away, again wanting more.

Chapter Fifteen

Meeting the Parents

"Dad, please be nice to Ken," I plead, standing in my parents' living room.

"I'm always nice," my dad says in his grumpy voice. "Your dress is too short. Go put some more clothes on." I begin to tug at the hem of my dress.

"She's not sixteen anymore, Ronald," my mom says to my dad.

"She looks like a prostitute," he says this like it's a fact and not his opinion.

I roll my eyes. "Dad, I'm standing right here!" He grumbles and goes back to watching *A Nightmare on Elm Street*, another one of his favorite 80s horror movies.

"Eva, stop pulling at your dress. You're making your cleavage hang out too much, but don't worry, you look beautiful," my mom tells me while holding Genesis in her lap. Genesis is drinking a bottle of milk and enjoying her time with her grandma.

I ignore my mom's comment about my boobs and accept her compliment, "Thanks, Mom. I appreciate it."

"So, where is Ken taking you?" she asks.

"I'm not sure where *Dr. Ken* is taking—"

My dad abruptly turns away from the television as Freddy claims another teenage victim. "What was that? Your boyfriend is a doctor?" Now I have my dad's undivided attention.

"Yes, he is an audiologist. He works at the same audiology department I take Genesis to," I say, proudly.

"Oh, that's lovely, Hunny," my mom says as her eyes light up. "So, where did you say he was going to take you tonight?"

"Uh, some restaurant. Someplace in San Diego. It's supposed to be the only Michelin Star restaurant nearby."

"Oh, my gosh. That sounds great, Eva," my mom says.

I pull out my phone to show my parents the picture I took while I was standing in Ken's driveway. My mom looks like she is going to faint, and I can see a smirk beginning to develop on my dad's face.

"What's the catch? No way the doctor can afford that house," my dad says, skeptical.

"Ken's dad was some major league baseball player,"

I start to explain. "Unfortunately, about a year ago, his parents passed away in a terrible car accident. They left him and his little sister everything."

My mom places her hand over her mouth. "Oh gosh, I think I saw something about that on the news a while back."

The doorbell rings, and everyone greets Ken at the door. I feel like my parents have pushed me out of the way like people do in a mosh pit to make it to the front of the stage.

"Hi, Mr. and Mrs. Gin. How are you doing this evening?" Ken says while standing outside at the front door.

"We are doing just fine. Oh, come on in," my mom instructs as she waves for him to enter.

"Thank you. It's nice to meet you both."

"You too, Son," my dad says, grinning widely.

Oh, here we go again, I think to myself. My dad aggressively grabs Ken's hand and starts shaking it up and down.

"Okay, Dad, you can let go of his hand now," I say while mouthing the word *sorry* to Ken.

"All right, well, let's go ahead and get out of here," I say, impatiently. I grab Ken's arm to pull him through the door before my parents do something else to embarrass me, but then I quickly turn back around, remembering to give Genesis a kiss goodbye. "Love you, my baby girl. Be good for grandma and grandpa." She waves bye.

Ken opens my door as I slide into his brand new Porsche. "Thank you," I say as I look at the leather interior.

"Sorry for the lack of space," he apologizes.

"Are you kidding me? This car is amazing," I say. I look out the window and notice everyone who is driving by slows down to check out Ken's car. "Luckily, I'm the size of an elf. So, I'm good," I say. Ken laughs at my joke.

"You really do look stunning tonight," he says as he reaches over to run his fingers through my straightened hair. His eyes are still focused on carefully driving me to the restaurant.

"Thank you. You look really handsome in your suit as well." I smile. "Oh, and thank you for picking me up at my parents' place. It really made it a lot easier for them and me. I would've had to drive back to Brandi's place or had to have my parents pick Genesis up."

"Of course, anything to help," he says, grabbing my hand.

We arrive at the restaurant and park next to all the other lavish sports cars. I begin to feel a little out of place. Ken sprints around the back of his car. He opens my door and grabs my hand to help me out. I wasn't used to this kind of care.

"Are you ready for one of the most outstanding meals of your life?" he asks, enthusiastically.

I wrap my arm around his bent elbow. "Yes! I cannot wait," I say, excitedly.

The main dining room floor is covered in crimson and pale-gold carpet. The chairs are oversized, meant for royalty. Spotless, white tablecloths cover every table. The grand brick fireplace sits in the middle of the room.

I begin to feel a bit disappointed that we aren't going to be dining in the main dining room. We continue on our way to the terrace. Once we are seated outside, my disappointment vanishes. The terrace overlooks an endless golf course, and the sun is just beginning to set. The sky is a lovely orange-red.

"Oh my gosh, Ken. This is so beautiful," I say as the waiter pulls my seat out and places a napkin on my lap. "So fancy."

"Just wait until you try the food. It's a prix fixe menu," he says.

"The anticipation is killing me! My mouth is already watering from all the hype. So, how many courses are we having?" I ask, anxiously.

"I ordered us the ten-course menu," he says. "But if

you still feel hungry after, we can order some more dishes."

"I don't think I will still be hungry after ten plates." I chuckle to myself.

The servers look so professional in their ivory shirts and black vests. They walk over to our table and bring us our first dish. "Amuse-bouche," they announce. The servers simultaneously place the tiny white bowls in front of Ken and me and list off the ingredients. "Iced yuzu, with honeydew, matcha, and yogurt." I wonder how many times they had to rehearse setting the dishes down in front of the diners at precisely the exact same moment. I look over at the table of six sitting diagonal to our table and watch as the six servers place the plates on the table, perfect and in sync.

I stare at the bowl filled with finely shaved green ice. It looks so fancy. "Is that real gold on there?" I point to the small, gold leaflet sitting on top of the yogurt.

"Yes," Ken answers. He is almost done with his first course. "It doesn't taste like anything. It's just for presentation."

"It looks too good to eat," I say as I take a small bite. "Mmm! Oh, wow, this is so good!"

"Yeah, and the courses keep getting better," Ken assures me.

"So, do you come here often?" I ask him.

"Not too often." He explains, "I've been here twice. The first time I ate at this restaurant was a month after my parents' accident, and the second time was when Emily came to visit me a couple of months ago. My father used to take my mother here on their anniversary. My mother used to say that there was no place better." This restaurant reminded Ken of his parents, especially his mom. They must have had a strong bond. I start to feel sorry for him again.

"I can see why she loved coming here." I smile at Ken.

"Yes, I think it reminded her of her restaurant days working as a sous-chef at a fine dining establishment... but enough about my family. Your mother and father seemed like nice people," Ken tells me.

"Yeah, they are really great parents," I say as the next course is presented to us. Every course is a perfect picture, painted on the dish. Every detail is carefully planned out and intentional. Every ingredient is fresh, flavorful, and exquisite. "I think you made a good impression on my parents tonight," I tell Ken. What I really wanted to say was the picture I showed them of your mansion made a good impression on my parents tonight. "Anyway, I don't think I will need to order any more food." I laugh. "I'm already getting so full, and we are only, what, a little over halfway done?" I say.

He smiles at me, neglecting my comment about my full stomach. "So, Eva, what are your plans for next week? Are you free?"

"Why do you ask?" I say, leaning in a little closer to Ken.

"I would like to take you to another restaurant that overlooks the harbor," he explains.

How could I say no? The food he is feeding me is like nothing I've ever had before.

This was when I realized *food is a form of persuasion.*

"Okay, you twisted my arm," I say, jokingly.

"So, Eva, tell me more about your goals in life and where you see yourself in ten years from now," he says. Wow, this is a serious question.

"Uh, well, I guess I haven't really thought that far out into my future," I say. I take a moment to think. "I guess my main goal in life is to raise a daughter who is intelligent and confident. I want Genesis to know she can be anything, do anything, achieve anything she wants when she grows up, no matter what anyone says about her. In ten years, I guess I see myself and Genesis in a place of our own. I see myself taking her to gymnastics practice or maybe piano lessons, whatever she's into at the time. I don't know," I say, shrugging my shoulders.

"Those are all wonderful goals. You are a good

mother, Eva," he says. "But what do you want in life for yourself? Do you see yourself marrying anytime soon?"

Oh, this is where the conversation is going. Oh, boy. "Uh, yeah, I mean if the guy is right for Genesis and me. Then yes, sure, I would love to get married. What about you? Where do you see yourself in ten years?"

"Well, I see myself with a family," he says, confidently. "A house full of my own kids running around and screaming." He begins to chuckle. I think he is lost in his daydream of his future family.

"So, how many kids do you want… exactly?" I ask, wondering if this is too intense of a question for a third date.

"I have always dreamed of having a large family, minimum of four kids. I had always thought it would've been nice to have more sisters or a brother," he explains.

I'm not sure I agree with Ken. I liked being a single child. I think one sibling would've been nice, but I also know that I would've gotten a lot less affection from my parents.

After two hours and ten courses later, we walk back to his car.

"Thank you for letting me take you out, Eva," he says.

"Are you kidding me? Thank *you* for the fantastic dinner. You were right. It was the best dinner I've ever had."

As we drive home, he puts his hand on my leg. "I'm so lucky to have met a fascinating woman like you. You are so beautiful," Ken says, flattering me.

I slowly push his hand up my thigh. Soon, his fingertips are under the short dress he had bought for me. I urge him to rub me.

He slowly retracts his hand from my thigh. "Eva, uh, I don't think I should do that," he says as he places his hand on the steering wheel. "I, um, don't want to get into an accident. Your parents wouldn't be very happy with me, now, would they?" Ken tries to joke.

I don't laugh and begin to feel embarrassed. What the hell? I think to myself. What does a girl have to do around here to get a little action?

"Oh, okay," I say, slightly angry.

"Eva, I apologize. I don't want to hurt your feelings. You're gorgeous. You really are." He looks at me for a brief second.

"No, it's fine," I lie. "I'm good." Rejection is the worst feeling in the world.

"Okay. I just think it might be a little soon in the relationship, you know?"

If we were ten years younger, I feel like this would've been a valid excuse. I don't understand.

"Wait, how many relationships have you had?"

Now he looks embarrassed. "Well, I've only had one serious relationship." He continues, "I met someone in medical school, and we dated for a couple of years. She ended up sleeping with another student in our class."

Now I understand. "Oh, what a bitch," I say. Hopeful, I might have lightened the mood. I feel much better after Ken's explanation.

"Yeah, she was a... bitch for doing that," he agrees. I can tell he still has some pent-up anger in his reserves. "And for also ruining me—permanently."

"What do you mean?" I ask.

"Well, physically, I guess. I'm not exactly comfortable with physical affection. She said that I wasn't fully satisfying her sexually, and that's why she cheated on me."

"Ugh, that's so terrible!" I say. "No, but really, that's messed up. She doesn't deserve someone like you. You know that, right?"

"Eh, I don't know," he says. I realize I had tapped into his insecurities.

"It's okay, Ken. There's no rush," I say, reassuring him. "I mean, I'm not dating you for your body. I'm dating you for the food that you're feeding me every weekend." We both laugh.

He nods his head, "Yes, okay." Ken looks less embarrassed now.

*****

We arrive at my parents' house to pick up Genesis, and Ken walks me to the front door.

"It appears that we have an audience," he says, pointing to the window. My dad and mom are staring at us through the blinds. They are kind of loud too. I can hear my mom telling my dad to scoot over because she can't see what's going on.

My hands fly over my face. "Oh, my gosh! My parents, they are something else."

He hugs me and gently kisses me on the lips. "I had a wonderful time tonight, Eva. I will see you next weekend." He walks back to his car, and I walk into my parents' house.

"Genesis is sleeping," my mom tells me. "How was dinner?"

"It was great, the best dinner I've ever had," I tell my mom. I take a minute and show her some of the pictures I took of the courses at dinner.

"The meals look so small," my mom mentions. "Do you want me to make you some noodles?"

"No, Mom. I'm actually pretty full." I smile at her. "Thank you, though. I should probably take Genesis home and get her into her bed."

As I walk out the door with my sleepy baby, my dad says, "You better make it work with that doctor of yours!"

Gee, no pressure. "Okay, Dad! Love you too!"

Chapter Sixteen

Mr. & Mrs. Young

"Well, if it isn't our favorite server," Mr. Young says.

"My favorite customers!" I say to Mr. Young and his wife. They are seated at their usual booth. "How are you both doing this afternoon?" I ask.

Mr. and Mrs. Young have been my favorite customers since I started working at Janette's.

They have also been married approximately five times longer than the time I've been employed at the cafe.

"We are doing good, Dearie," Mrs. Young says. She brushes her silvery hair away from her eyes.

"New hairdo?" I ask Mrs. Young.

"Oh, yes. I got it done this morning," she replies

and bounces the bottom of her curly hair with her palm.

"It looks great," I say.

"How is Genesis doing?" Mrs. Young asks.

"She's doing good, just hanging out with her grandma and grandpa today until I get off of work."

"Is she walking yet?" Mrs. Young asks.

"No, not quite, but she's almost there. My guess is she will probably be walking shortly after her birthday. It's coming up soon."

Mr. and Mrs. Young currently have five children, twelve grandchildren, and one great-granddaughter that's on the way.

"How is your family doing?" I ask.

"Oh, they are good. Our grandson and his wife want to name their baby girl Amethyst. Isn't that some kind of stone or something?" Mr. Young asks.

"Uh, I believe so," I say.

"Well, whatever happened to simple names like Ethel or Florence or Mary?" Mr. Young asks.

"My grandma's name was Mary," I tell Mr. and Mrs. Young.

"See, now that's a beautiful name," Mr. Young claims.

I chuckle. "Should I bring you two decaf coffees and two waters?"

"Yup," Mr. Young answers. "You got it."

"Okay, I will be right back with your drink order."

As I make my way over to Mr. and Mrs. Young's table with the coffees and waters, my walking pace starts to slow. I notice the couple holding hands like they always do on the Wednesdays that I work. They begin to laugh at something humorous Mr. Young has said, and they continue with their intimate conversation. Then, I see Mr. Young lean in and give Mrs. Young a long, passionate kiss. Even after almost five decades of marriage, they still have plenty to talk about. They still hold each other's hands. They still share a heartfelt kiss, and they still find things to laugh about.

I set their drinks down on the table. "So, Eva, are you planning on going back to school to finish your studies?" Mr. Young asks me.

"Yeah, maybe. We will see," I respond, knowing I probably won't. "I've just been preoccupied with my little lady. It's definitely a full-time job being a mom."

A few months before I graduated high school, I had told my parents that I wanted to take a couple years off from school before going to college. I wasn't quite sure what I wanted to study anyway. My mom and dad weren't exactly enthralled with my choice and told me that I needed to get a job if I wasn't taking classes. Shortly after I received my high school diploma, I began working at Janette's. Eventually, I started taking a couple classes each semester at the local community college. A couple years prior to Genesis being born, I earned my associate degree in general studies. From there, I still hadn't really decided where I wanted to take my education. I became comfortable at the cafe and really enjoyed my job. I thought about going to a four-year college, but the tuition was so expensive. My parents had suggested I apply for some grants, which I ended up doing, mostly to stop them from bugging me, but I didn't have any luck. A year or two before Genesis was born, Liam had told me we would be fine if I kept working part-time at the cafe, and he would support us as long as I took care of all the housework. It seemed like a fair deal to me at the time. Then, once I had Genesis, she had become my priority, and the likelihood of me furthering my education was a distant thought.

"I'm just asking because I don't want to lose our favorite server," Mr. Young explains.

Mr. and Mrs. Young always over-tip me. I'm so grateful for their kindness, but I can't help but think that they are a little concerned about Genesis and my financial well-being.

I smile warmly at Mr. Young and then at his wife. "Would you both like the usual today?" I ask.

"How did you know?" Mrs. Young says, sarcastically.

"All right, I will have that right up for you." As I begin to walk away from the table, I quickly turn around and ask, "Do you mind if I ask you both a question?"

"Oh, of course not, Dearie," Mrs. Young says. "What is it?"

"Well, I want to know, since, you know, you both still look so happy, even after forty-nine years of marriage. What's your secret?"

They both start to chuckle. "Ah, well, Eva"—Mr. Young starts to say—"I wouldn't say it's a secret, but you know, there's a lot to it."

"Here, sit down next to us for a few minutes, Eva," Mrs. Young says as she pats the seat next to her.

I look around. "Okay, just for a couple minutes. I don't think it's too busy." I slide into the booth and sit next to Mrs. Young, anxious to hear her answer.

"Is there a boy?" Mrs. Young whispers into my ear. She may be old, but she's as sharp as a tack.

I nod my head. "Yeah, we've been on a few dates. My parents really like him," I explain.

Mrs. Young's face brightens. "Oh, that's wonderful, Dearie!" she says.

"So, do *you* really like him?" Mr. Young asks.

"Well, yeah. I mean, he's taken me on a couple of

really nice dates, and he's super sweet and responsible."

Mr. Young makes a disgusted face like he just sucked on a lemon. "*Responsible?* You want to be with someone who is *responsible?*" he asks.

"Oh, ignore him," Mrs. Young says as her hand makes contact with the back of her husband's head. Mr. Young didn't flinch. He must've been used to it. I can't help but laugh. "Have you kissed him yet?" Mrs. Young nosily asks.

"Yeah, Mrs. Young. We've kissed a couple times."

"Have you two had sex?" Mrs. Young nosily asks... again.

My jaw drops open wide. I can't believe Mrs. Young is asking me if I had sex with Ken. My face turns bright red. "Uh, no, we, uh—" I stammer.

"It's okay, Dearie," she says. She pats me on the middle of my back. "I was just curious. That has nothing to do with what I want to tell you."

Oh, my gosh, I think to myself. Old people can get away with almost anything! "Um, okay," I say, confused.

"When Mr. Young first kissed me, I felt something like I've never felt before," she explains. "Mr. Young pulled me in close to his robust body, looked straight into my eyes, and kissed the heck out of me. It had to have been over ten minutes before we surfaced for air."

This is so awkward but also so adorable at the same

time. "Wow." I nod my head. "Ten minutes, huh?" We all start to laugh. "That's a long time," I say, stating the obvious.

"She was so beautiful, a perfect angel, carved directly from God's hands," Mr. Young says. He holds his hands above the table and outlines the curves of a woman's body. "I just couldn't resist her… I still can't resist her," Mr. Young says and leans toward Mrs. Young for another long kiss. They start to make out uncontrollably on the cafe booth. They wrap their arms around one another, and I think I see some fog collect on Mr. Young's glasses.

"Okay, well, I, uh, think I'd better go put your order in," I say, excusing myself from the table. Mr. and Mrs. Young are oblivious to my absence and continue kissing one another.

Janette walks out of the kitchen to see how many diners have filled the dining room this afternoon. She spots Mr. and Mrs. Young eagerly making out in her restaurant. "Oh, looks like they are at it again," she says and walks back into the kitchen.

I look over my shoulder at the couple, and I begin to yearn for a taste of their passion.

Chapter Seventeen

Too Tight

"Crap, crap, crap!" I say to myself as I attempt to get dressed for my date tonight.

"What are you doing in there, Eva?" Brandi asks from the living room.

"I'm stuck! Can you come help me? Please! Hurry!" I yell from the bathroom.

Brandi walks in and sees me almost butt naked, attempting to pull my dress over my head. I stand in front of her in a lacy black thong and matching bra.

"Nice lingerie," Brandi says, mocking me.

"Help me pull my dress down," I say. My voice is muffled by the dress that's covering my entire face, and my hands are permanently stuck upward in the air.

"Why did you try to pull it over your head? Usually, you are supposed to step into the dress and pull it up over your body," Brandi explains.

135

"I know, I know! I tried that. It didn't work. I couldn't get it past my hips. I thought I would give this a shot and see if I could slide it on this way," I say, frustrated.

Curvier hips were a gift from being pregnant with Genesis, and so were larger hands and bigger feet, but that didn't matter right this moment.

Brandi helps shimmy my bright red dress down over my shoulders. "Okay, I think I've got it," she says.

"Okay, now help me zip up my dress," I say while turning my back toward Brandi.

Brandi rolls her eyes at me. "Okay, suck it in," she instructs and successfully zips up the back of my dress but not with ease. I can hardly breathe comfortably. I think I hear Genesis jumping up and down in her bouncer, also laughing at me.

"Why's your dress so tight?" Brandi asks as I pick up the straightener to style my hair.

"I ordered it online a couple days ago. The dress runs a little small. I should've checked the sizing chart before buying it, but I didn't think about it at the time. I just got the dress yesterday in the mail. It was too late to exchange it for a larger size."

"You could've just borrowed one of my dresses," Brandi says nicely.

"In case you haven't noticed, you're tall like a

model, and I'm short like a dwarf," I remind her. "All your dresses would be way too long on me."

"Good point... Trying to look sexy for Dr. Grayson, are we now?" Brandi asks.

She is staring at me in the mirror with her hands on her hips. "You guys gonna bone tonight?" She winks at my reflection. She starts making kissy faces and then starts to dry hump the air, pumping her bent arms back and forth in the opposite motion of her hips. Now her facial expressions look straight up raunchy.

I shove her out of the bathroom. "Thank you, but your services are no longer required." We both laugh.

I finish applying my makeup, adding a little more than I have been on my previous dates with Ken. I wish what Brandi had said was true. I wish Ken wanted to make endless love to me. I wish he wanted me to kiss his neck and fully satisfy him, but I had to remember to be patient.

Although, I do guiltily admit, I ordered the lingerie and the dress with hopeful thinking in mind. Maybe he will change his mind tonight, or maybe he will be more comfortable around me this go around. Maybe, just maybe, we will *bone* tonight.

"You look nice, Eva," Max says as I walk out of the bathroom.

"Oh, hi! I didn't hear you sneak in. Thanks," I say,

surprised. He gives me a warm hug, and I think of how Max is such a sweet guy.

When Brandi first introduced me to Max, about a month after they found each other online, I couldn't stop staring at his unfit body and short stature. I wondered how Max managed to go indoor rock climbing with Brandi, another one of her hobbies. I pictured him strapped into a harness and out of breath as he struggled to make it up the wall.

I kept trying to compare Max's and Brandi's height difference every time they stood close enough to one another. Once I was able to gauge that Max was about an inch shorter than Brandi, I understood why her high heels were shoved to the back of her closet for the last four weeks.

Before I met Max, I pictured him as a six-foot-two, seductive nurse. I imagined his chiseled arms, busting out of his uniform, pleading for a larger pair of scrubs as he helped lift his patient onto a wheelchair. I thought he would look like all the other athletic guys Brandi dated in high school and college, but my assumptions were incorrect. Max wasn't extremely chubby, but he definitely looked more like a person who played video games the majority of his free time rather than spending it on a boogie board in the ocean. Also, Max was only a couple years older than us, but his shaven head and apricot-red goatee made him look a few years older than he actually was.

It wasn't until he asked to take Genesis from my arms so he could hold her that he started to look more attractive. Max began telling me how cute my daughter was, and I realized how beautiful a person he was. He told me Brandi had mentioned to him how fast Genesis had been growing out of her clothes and handed me a bag with outfits he handpicked for Genesis. At that moment, I felt like the most shallow person I had ever known.

"Brandi mentioned something about you going on a date tonight, and she suggested we spend our night off together at her place and babysit Genesis," Max says.

"Yeah, I should be back in a couple hours. Thank you for helping with Genesis tonight."

Genesis smiles at Max and raises her arms, asking him to pick her up. He grabs Genesis from her bouncer and sits back down on the couch with Brandi. "Of course, she's such an easy baby," he responds. I'm glad he thinks so.

"Oh, congratulations, by the way. I don't think I've seen you since you and Brandi got engaged!"

"Thanks. Yeah, it's been a little while since I've seen

you and Genesis," he says.

"Well, I cannot wait for the wedding," I say to them as I finish gathering my things.

I arrive at Ken's, and he greets me at the door. "Sorry you had to drive over to my place tonight. I wanted to pick you up, but my sister called, and I got stuck on the phone talking to her for longer than I had predicted.

"Oh, Emily? Is everything all right with her?" I ask, concerned.

"Yes, she's okay. She's just been a little down lately, thinking about our mom and dad's accident," he explains while putting his dress shoes on. "Next Sunday will be exactly a year since their accident."

"Oh, my gosh. It's totally fine, Ken. I completely understand," I say. "I didn't mind driving over here at all."

"Thanks, Eva. Let's get going before we are late for our reservation," he says. Ken puts his hand on the back of my waist and escorts me out to his car.

Once we pull out of the driveway, Ken sets his hand on my thigh. For a brief moment, I am tempted to slide his fingers under my dress, but instead, I start to think about the last time he denied me. I place my hand on the top of his and decide I won't pressure him tonight.

"Hey, so, would your sister be willing to come down to San Diego next weekend?" I ask, curiously.

"Uh, possibly. Why do you ask?"

"Well, Genesis turns one in three days, and my parents want to throw her a birthday party. It's going to be at their house this next Saturday," I explain.

"One-year-old, huh?" he says, excitedly.

"Well, what if Emily comes down for the weekend, and we can all go to my parents' to celebrate Genesis' birthday?" I ask, hopeful. "I really want to meet her."

"Okay, you know what? That sounds really nice. I bet Emily would like that a lot." Ken seems pleased with my suggestion. "I will give Emily a call tomorrow and let you know."

The harbor looks beautiful at night. We sit down at the restaurant table that is pushed up against the window. The restaurant's walls are lined with clear glass, from the top of the ceiling to the bottom of the floor, and I can see the dazzling hotel lights across the calm water.

"The food here is delicious but not as good as our last dinner," he tells me. "But the view is something else, as you can see."

"Yeah, the view is perfect," I say, agreeing with him. "Thank you for spoiling me rotten the last three weekends. It's been really amazing."

We hold each other's hands. I lean across the table and give him a short kiss on his lips, making sure not to linger too long. I don't want him to feel like I am pursuing him too quickly. I think back to the conversation I had a few days ago with Mr. and Mrs. Young. I think of their undeniable passion for one another and their never-ending make out session on the restaurant booth. I think of how that will never be Ken and me.

When we return to Ken's house, he doesn't invite me in. I know it has everything to do with the conversation we had last weekend in his car. Surprisingly, he kisses me for almost a full minute before I leave. I suppose this is satisfactory, a baby step above our last goodbye kiss. I drive home, thinking of how I wasted my money on trashy lingerie.

"Ugh! Sasuke! You are so naughty Mr. Wiener!" I scream as I sit in an enormous pile of dog pee. Sasuke is standing in front of me, heavily panting and wagging his tail. He had peed in his favorite spot by the front door. I had slipped and fallen in the puddle when I returned home from Ken's house. "Bad Wienie! Bad! Wienie!" I yell at him as I pick myself up off the floor. Sasuke tucks his tail and runs to his dog bed.

"Brandi! Your dog peed all over the floor—"

"Hi, Eva," Brian says.

Oh, shit. It's Brandi's younger brother. He's gotten really tall and handsome since the last time I saw him. "Brian Ryan? Where are Brandi and Max?" I ask, surprised to see him holding Genesis. That's what I used to call him back in our high school days, Brian Ryan.

Brian was a freshman during Brandi's and my junior year of high school. I remember the first day of school. I had bumped into Brian on my way to class. "Hi, Brian Ryan, are you lost?" I asked him. Brian was standing in the hallway with a handful of books that looked a bit too heavy for him. He struggled, carrying his books in his scrawny arms, which were the same diameter as mine.

"I'm looking for room 12," he said while timidly, scanning the large campus.

"Okay, I know where that is. I can take you over there," I said. "Come on, Brian Ryan, let's go." We began walking toward his classroom, and I noticed that his backpack also looked like it was weighing him down. "Tough first day of high school, huh?" I asked.

"Yeah, just a little," he replied. "So, how have you been?"

"Not too bad," I said. "Pretty excited for my first day back." Brian still looked a little nervous. "Don't worry, Brian Ryan. It'll get better. Once you learn your way around it will be a lot—"

"What the heck are you doing, Brian?" Brandi said while she angrily walked up to us. "I told you, no talking to anybody that I know!" She looked around to see who else was watching, clearly embarrassed by her younger brother.

Then, she quickly yanked me in the opposite direction toward our art class. I tried to turn around as I was being dragged down the hall by Brandi. "It's over there, Brian Ryan," I tried to scream and point Brandi's little brother in the right direction. He looked like a normal, intimidated, lost freshman—a lost little puppy dog.

"Max's mom had an emergency. I think she fell down the stairs or something and had to go to the hospital. She hit her head pretty good and might've fractured her wrist," Brian explains. "Brandi wanted to go with him, but she thought it would've been a little late to drop off Genesis at your parents. I only live about five minutes away, so, I rushed over here when she called."

"Oh, uh, okay. Well, hopefully Max's mom is doing okay. Thank you for coming over to watch Genesis on such short notice."

"Yeah, she didn't want to ruin your date," he says.

"Oh, no. Let me go put Genesis down." Brian spots the puddle of dog pee and my revealing, tight-fitting, ruined dress. "Sorry, I didn't realize he had to go outside." Now Brian is staring at my generous cleavage popping out above my dress.

"Yeah, it's fine. He's really bad about having accidents," I say, reassuring him. Brian walks over to set Genesis in her bouncer and turns on *Beauty and the Beast* to keep her occupied. He shuffles through the closet and finds a towel.

"Thank you," I say as he hands me the towel to clean myself up a bit.

"No worries. Sorry again," he apologizes. "Why don't you go take a shower or something, and I will clean up the mess."

"Are you sure?" I ask. "I don't mind cleaning it—"

"No, I got it. Go ahead and get yourself cleaned up," Brian instructs.

"All right," I say and quickly walk to the bathroom. Before I close the bathroom door, I peek out and see Brian soaking up the dog pee with a handful of paper towels. I think of how chivalrous he's become. Maybe that's a slight exaggeration, but a kind man, nonetheless.

I shut the bathroom door and look in the mirror. Dog pee has completely saturated the back of my dress. So gross. I pull my hair to the side of my neck and try to unzip my dress. "Dammit!" I say as I fail at pulling the zipper down. I spend a good five minutes trying to get undressed, contorting my arms in uncomfortable positions behind my back. I stand in my dog pee dress, defeated.

"Brian!" I yell from the bathroom. I peek my head out of the door. He had just finished cleaning up Sasuke's accident. "Uh, do you think... you could possibly... help me undo my zipper?" I ask, hesitantly.

"Uh, sure," he says. "I think I can, um, manage that." He joins me in the bathroom.

"I ordered too small a dress, and now it's stuck," I try to explain my predicament as I awkwardly stand in front of Brian.

Brian struggles to unzip my dress. "Just try to squeeze the top of the dress when you pull the zipper down." I try to coach him while pinching my shoulder blades closer together.

"Got it!" he says, proudly.

I can feel him slowly pull the zipper down my back, ending at the bottom of my lacy thong. I quickly and vigorously yank down the dress past my hips, excited not to be covered in dog pee. For a brief moment, I had forgotten that Brian was still standing behind me. My dress had dropped onto the floor, and now I am standing in my lingerie meant for Ken. I'm standing in

146

the sensual lingerie that was meant to be taken off by Ken's hands before we made love to one another.

Brian places his fingertips on the bottom of my neck and slowly begins to draw a path down my spine. As his hand passes over my bra, goosebumps form, invading the surface of my entire body. His fingertips continue down the arch of my lower back. My breathing quickens, and my heart begins to pound, about to break out of my chest. I close my eyes as his path ends at the top of my panties. I can no longer feel his gentle touch. I breathe in deeply and turn to face him. Our eyes meet. For a moment, I am entranced by his dark brown eyes. I am distracted by his masculine build. I lift my hand to touch his muscles on the side of his arm, exposed by the tank top he is currently wearing. My eyes are averted to his sensual lips, tempting me. I am enticed by his height. Brian is tall, dark, and handsome. He was no longer the same scrawny freshman that I knew in high school.

"Oh, I'm sorry," he says as he quickly turns and exits the bathroom. He bumps into the doorframe on his way out, hitting the side of his arm. He pauses in place, puts his opposite hand on the arm he rammed into the doorframe, and continues to walk out of the bathroom like he didn't just awkwardly run into a wall.

I close the door, slip off my lingerie, and start the shower. I am confused about what just happened. Did I want Brian's hands to replace Ken's hands and rip off my lingerie? Did I want Brian's hands to replace Ken's hands as they discover all the curves of my body?

As I step into the warm water pouring down from above, I begin fantasizing about Brian joining me in the shower. I imagine that my hands are pressed against the tile on the wall. My body is slightly bent over, and my back is arched as I let him take advantage of me from behind. I imagine the water running down our naked bodies as I moan from pure pleasure. His hands are firmly placed on my hips, helping him peak to ecstasy.

After I'm done fantasizing in the shower, I realize I had forgotten to grab clothes to change into. Shoot! I wrap my towel around my body and tuck the corner of the towel underneath my arm. I, again, peek out of the bathroom.

"Uh, Brian, I forgot to grab my clothes," I say to him awkwardly. He is sitting on the couch watching the movie with Genesis. Genesis is still in her bouncer, bouncing away happily as she sucks on one of her baby fingers.

He looks at me. "Oh, did you want me to grab you something to wear?"

He starts to get up from the couch, but the thought of him looking at and fingering my stash of panties makes me feel uneasy. "Um, no, I can get it. Just close your eyes for a minute."

He laughs. "But I just saw you in your bra and underwear fifteen minutes ago."

"I don't care that you saw me half-naked fifteen minutes ago! Just cover your eyes!" I yell at him, still hiding behind the bathroom door.

"Oh gosh, Eva. Okay," he says, and he slowly brings his hands to his eyelids. "There, my eyes are closed now."

I quickly scamper over to collect my clothes, holding my bath towel against my body with one hand. I hurriedly reach into the plastic drawer that I am temporarily storing my undergarments in while staying at Brandi's, you know, one of those plastic organizers sometimes used for art supplies and whatnot. As I search for a pair of underwear that's more comfortable than my previous one—preferably one that doesn't give me a permanent wedgie for the rest of the night—my towel slips from under my arm, revealing one of my boobs.

"Your eyes still closed?" I scream, slightly panicking while quickly pulling the towel back over my naked breast.

"Yes, they are still closed," Brian says, annoyed. "Are you almost done?" I'm pretty sure I saw him peek through his fingers once or twice while I scampered around the living room, collecting my clothes. Though, I doubt Brian would ever admit it.

"Okay! You can open your eyes now!" I yell while I begin dressing in the bathroom.

I walk out into the living room in a much more comfy outfit—my pair of stained leggings and an oversized shirt I often wore when I was pregnant with Genesis. I ask Brian if he had already gotten something to eat, hoping he also remembered to feed Genesis dinner.

He looks at me hesitantly. "Genesis and I ate almost all the fried rice that was in the fridge… and maybe the chow mein too," he says. I smile as I picture him enjoying the fried rice with my daughter. "It was so good! Best fried rice I've ever had, hands down. I hope it was okay that I helped myself."

"Oh, of course," I assure him. "Although, if I don't replenish what you guys ate within the next couple days, Brandi will have my ass."

"She's lucky to have her own personal cook living with her," he flatters me.

"Ass!" Genesis repeats. "Ass!" she says a second time but more confident.

I look at Brian as he removes Genesis from her bouncer. He's laughing hysterically. My hands slap the front of my face as I cover my regret.

I shake my head. "I shouldn't have said that," I say

as an awkward laugh escapes from my body.

"She must be in that stage where she repeats everything you say," Brian says through his laughter.

"Yeah," I reply. I think my cheeks are flushed from my embarrassment. "Usually, I'm more careful with my word choices," I claim.

"Don't stress too much," Brian reassures me. "Luckily, at this age, they also tend to forget the word as soon as they say it."

This is true. Unless I consistently repeat the same word over and over again to Genesis, she typically doesn't remember the word the next day. I smile at Brian. He's turned into such a cordial man. I feel better but still hope she won't repeat my bad language tomorrow.

"You think it would be okay if Genesis and I finish watching our movie before I leave?" Brian asks.

I look at the time. It's thirty minutes before her normal bedtime. "Of course," I reply. I'm glad he is going to stay a while longer.

I notice the kitchen sink is stacked full, and I head over to defeat the ridiculously large pile of dishes. So many dishes created throughout the day by Brandi, Brian, Genesis, and me. I tie up my damp hair into a messy bun and prepare myself for a ten-minute round of dishwashing.

I glance at the movie and see that my favorite scene is playing. Belle and the Beast are gracefully walking down the stairs, preparing to perform their famous dance together in the glorious castle ballroom.

"This is my favorite part," I point out to Brian.

I pause from scrubbing the dishes to stare at the TV screen. Belle and the Beast start dancing, but my eyes have somehow made their way from the TV to Brian and Genesis. Genesis is sitting gleefully on Brian's lap. He starts to sing the lyrics to *Beauty and the Beast* and gently begins to sway Genesis back and forth on his legs. I hear Genesis' sweet baby giggles. Her laughter is endless. My heart melts at the sight of Brian serenading my beautiful girl. I smile to myself, thinking it's possible Brian is enjoying himself more than Genesis.

"So, Brian, what have you been up to these days?" I ask from Brandi's open kitchen.

"Uh, not too much," he replies. "Just living the single life. I bought a condo a few months ago. It's just a few minutes from Brandi's place," he reminds me.

A smile consumes my face, realizing he had confirmed he isn't currently seeing anyone. "That's awesome!" I reply. "It's a pretty nice neighborhood over here."

"What about you? Besides taking care of Genesis and going on dates? Are you still working at the cafe?"

he inquires.

"Yeah, I've just been working there part-time while I raise my little girly. Janette's been more than generous with working around Genesis' doctor appointments. She even makes an effort to give me most weekends off. I really enjoy working there. The regulars are always so fun to talk to," I say as I finally start to rinse the dishes.

"I haven't been to Janette's yet. How's the food there?"

"It's really great. I mean, I like it," I respond.

"You will have to take me on a date there some time," he says.

The sudsy bowl I hold in my hand falls into the bottom of the sink and clanks loudly against the other dishes. "Whoops," I say, thinking about going on a date with Brandi's not-so-little brother.

"You good over there?" Brian asks while watching Belle and the Beast complete their dance with one another. *Must be his favorite part too*, I think to myself.

"Yeah, I'm good," I say, and I continue to finish washing the dishes less clumsily. "So, what are you currently doing for work?" I ask.

"I actually got hired on by a police department shortly after high school. I completed the academy about four years back," he explains.

I guess that would explain his militaresque type of

haircut. I think it's called a high and tight? His light brown hair is faded, fairly short on the sides and back, but the top is longer and combed over to one side. I guess that would also explain his baby-shaven face that exposes his square-shaped jawline. His features are attractive. He could be one of those male underwear models in one of the catalogs I look through, more often than I probably should.

"Oh, same department that your dad worked at?" I ask, remembering that Brandi's dad was a police sergeant.

"No, a different one, but he put in a good word for me," he explains.

"I bet your parents were jumping up and down when they found out that both of their children were going to follow in their footsteps," I mention.

"Yeah, they were pretty happy. I mean, they were really ecstatic," Brian confirms.

"Well, your job sounds like fun... I think? Actually, I guess it's probably pretty tough work."

"Yeah, at times, it can be stressful. It's pretty neat, though, because I don't just patrol the streets like at most departments. Sometimes, I get to drive a boat around the harbor, and other days I help monitor the airport."

"I bet you meet a lot of *interesting* people," I say.

Brian nods his head. "Yeah, definitely, but I love it. There's never a dull day."

"Is it hard to stay fit for the job?" I ask. My eyes are drawn to his wide, muscular shoulders and biceps again.

"We actually have our own gym at the station. It's pretty nice. It makes it easy to work out before and after my shift," he explains.

Before and after his shift? That's a lot of time spent working out, but by the looks of it, it has most definitely paid off.

Brian picks Genesis up off his lap and brings her over to the changing table. "What do you want me to put her in for bed?" he asks.

"Oh, I'll get it," I say as I dry my wet hands on my baggy shirt.

"It's okay. You're busy. I just don't know where you keep her pajamas," he says.

"It's all right. I'm pretty much done with dishes." I grab Genesis' sleeper off the rack of clothes. I walk over to the changing table and hand him Genesis' footie pajamas. I expect to see Brian struggle while changing my daughter's diaper, but I am more than surprised at his diaper skills. "Where did you learn to change a diaper?" I ask Brian as he takes Genesis' sleeper from my hands.

He begins putting my squirmy daughter into her pajamas. "You know how Brandi always babysat Carly during the summer months?" he asks.

"Yeah, I think so. The little girl with super curly hair that lived on the end of your parents' cul-de-sac?" I recall. "The girl that Brandi watched for three years or so?"

"Yeah, exactly. Well, Brandi used to give me a commission for every diaper that needed to be changed, so she wouldn't have to do it. She tried to change Carly's diaper one time and decided it was too disgusting a job. Funny she turned out to be a nurse, huh?"

"I think almost all teenagers have a tough time dealing with human poop. I still haven't gotten over my fear of baby poop," I say, giggling. "I still fight dry heaves while changing Genesis' loaded diapers."

"Anyway, Brandi started upping my baby responsibilities," Brian explains. "She refused to pay me more, even though I was pretty much watching Carly on my own."

"Oh, my gosh. I guess you got the short end of the stick on that deal," I say. "Sounds like something a big sister would do to her younger brother." Our laughter swarms the room.

"Yeah. When we were younger, she also tricked me into doing a lot of her chores around the house," he says. He starts to mix the formula in Genesis' bottle.

I nod my head. "I bet she did," I reply, and our

laughter starts to fade.

"Do you want me to take her?" I ask Brian, holding my arms out.

He starts to feed Genesis her milk. "Nah, I got it. She's an easy baby," he says while rocking her back and forth. She becomes sleepy, nestled comfortably in Brian's arms. "Well, she almost made it to the end of the movie," he says as he looks into my daughter's tired eyes and smiles.

"Yeah, it's a little bit past her bedtime," I mention.

Brian sets Genesis down in her crib. She is now fast asleep. I take her hearing aid out and place it in its case.

"Oh, I forgot about that," Brian says. "Brandi had mentioned I needed to take out Genesis' hearing aid if she fell asleep before you got home."

"No worries. I've had lots of practice. It's just part of my daily routine now." I smile at him. "Thank you for putting her to sleep for me," I say, taking the empty bottle from his hand.

"Of course. I'm glad I was able to come over tonight. It was fun hanging out with Genesis and seeing you."

"You too, Brian. It's been way too long!" I say, not wanting our conversation to end.

He wraps his strong arms around my petite body and squeezes me a little too tight. Tighter than friendly hugs tend to be. Tighter than *family friend* hugs usually tend to be. His chin softly rests on the top of my head. I feel safe in his arms and completely forget about Ken. He lets go of me sooner than I would've liked.

"Hey, so, maybe I can take you out this next Saturday?" Brian asks. "I only have weekends off for a few more weeks until my schedule changes."

"I would really like that, but my parents are throwing Genesis a birthday party that day," I explain.

"Oh, okay. No worries. Maybe another day." Brian looks discouraged. "I can't believe she's almost one!" he says, trying to disguise his disappointment.

"I know, it's so crazy. It seriously blows my mind," I say. "Well, why don't you come over and celebrate with us? I'm sure my parents would love seeing you after all these years," I suggest.

"Okay, that sounds good," Brian says, excitedly. "I will see you next week then."

"I will be looking forward to seeing you again!" I say as he walks out the door.

I close the door behind Brian, shut my eyes, and begin to think about him running his fingers down my back again.

My eyes quickly shoot open. "Oh, gosh, what have I done?" I say to myself, remembering that Ken will be at Genesis' birthday party too. Crap!

Chapter Eighteen

Birthday Girl

"Hi Brian!" my mom says as she gives him a warm hug. "Oh, my goodness. You've grown up! I barely recognized you."

"Hi, Mrs. Gin. It's nice to see you," he tells my mom.

"It's been a long, long time." My mom grabs his bulging tricep with her hand. "You have become a strong man," she says, shaking his muscular arm back and forth in her viselike grip. Brian chuckles awkwardly and looks at me silently, begging for help.

"Okay, Mom. That's enough. Let Brian go," I say. She eventually releases her grip.

"Brian!" my dad says, joining our conversation. My dad shakes Brian's hand solidly. "How are things going with your parents?"

My parents had become pretty good friends with

Brandi's parents over the past fourteen years of Brandi's and my friendship. We had endless sleepovers at each other's houses. My parents would always check with Brandi's parents to make sure I was *actually* going to stay the night at their house. My word wasn't enough during my high school years. They wanted to make sure I wasn't snorting cocaine in some random dude's car or lying in a ditch somewhere. I would never want to disappoint my parents, so the likelihood of that ever happening was non-existent.

"They are doing good. My dad finally retired a couple of years ago," Brian says.

"That's good to hear. Your sister told me that you became an officer too," my dad says.

"Yeah, I've been an officer for—"

"Oh! Hi Ken!" my mom screams as Ken walks up to join our group conversation. My mom is way too excited to see Ken. She gives him a long hug, squeezing him tightly. She's probably thinking about the picture again—the one I showed her on my phone of Ken's multi-million-dollar mansion.

"Hi, Mr. and Mrs. Gin," he says while holding out his hand to properly greet my father.

My dad quickly grabs Ken's hand and shakes it firmly. He even pulls him in for a hug. "Good to see you again, Son," he says, smiling at Ken.

I've never heard my dad call anyone *Son* before he had met Ken. So weird.

"This is my sister, Emily," Ken says, introducing his sister.

"Emily!" I say, enthusiastically. I give her a warm hug. "Thank you for driving all the way down from L.A. It's so nice to finally meet you!"

Emily's hair is just as dark and beautiful as Ken's. Her eyes are more of a gray rather than a blue like her brother's. I think back to their perfect family portrait hanging above their fireplace and wonder how it would look with Genesis and me in the picture. I wasn't positive we would fit in.

"Of course. I had to come and meet my brother's girlfriend. He won't stop texting me. Every conversation has you in it," Emily says, kindly.

"Only good things, though, right?" I say to Emily, jokingly.

She nods while placing her hands on the sides of my shoulders. We both are laughing, "Yes, of course, only good things—Oh! Is that your adorable birthday girl over there?" Emily points to Genesis happily playing with her cousin on the carpet in my parents' living room. I dressed her in a fluffy, sparkly, peony dress.

"Yeah, that's my little princess," I confirm.

"She's so beautiful, Eva." She walks over and sits

down beside Genesis. They start to converse while Emily picks up a ball and rolls it on the floor to Genesis.

My mom and dad have pulled Ken aside, and the three of them are having their own private pow-wow.

"So, boyfriend, huh?" Brian asks, looking me in the eyes.

"Oh, uh—I would hardly call him my boyfriend. We've only been on three dates," I try to convince him while breaking our eye contact.

"Uh-huh, okay," Brian says as we each pick up a paper plate to fill with Chinese food. "I see how it is. You undress right in front of me and tempt me with your irresistible body, only for me to find out you are already taken," he says, jokingly—possibly semi-seriously.

"Like I said, we've only gone on a handful of dates," I try to persuade him. "And we've only kissed a handful of times." I place a fried dumpling on my plate.

"Okay, if you say so, Eva," he playfully bumps the side of my arm with his. "Sure looks like your parents are pretty fond of him." We both pause to look at my parents and Ken, chatting away in their own personal corner.

"Yeah… they sure are," I say.

"Oh man! There is enough food here to feed hundreds of people," Brian mentions. He continues to gather food onto his plate. There are long tables lined up next to each other in my mom and dad's dining room with a dozen warming trays in a neat row with various types of Chinese food. It basically is a Chinese buffet set up in my parents' house.

"Yeah, my mom always says, 'If you have just enough food to feed all of your guests, then you didn't provide enough food.' See, my mom even stacked little to-go containers over there," I say, pointing to the boxes set on the end of the table. They are similar to the take-out boxes you see at Chinese restaurants. "So, you will also have lunch and dinner for the next three days."

"Sweet!" he replies. "So, this is how it always is for birthdays?"

"Yeah, pretty much—birthdays, graduations, weddings, and basically every holiday."

Food is an important part of my family's culture. There's no point in having a gathering or a party of any kind unless copious amounts of food are served. Providing food for family and friends is a way of showing you are happy they came to celebrate. Filling your guests' stomachs is a way of being a gracious host.

This was when I realized *food is a form of celebration.*

Ken eventually notices that I am still hanging out

and talking with Brian, who clearly doesn't look related to me. Ken walks over to interrupt our playful conversation.

"Sorry, Eva. I got caught up talking to your parents. They wanted to know more about how I got into the medical field," he says, glancing at Brian.

"Ah, medical field?" Brian asks him. I think Brian might be trying to compare himself to his competition.

"Yes, I am an audiologist. I was lucky enough to bump into Eva at one of Genesis' appointments," he says to Brian.

"Oh, you got yourself a doctor, huh, Eva?" Brian awkwardly says to me. I feel like his comment is directed more toward Ken, but he looked at me when he said it.

"Yes," Ken nods. "I also came to Eva's rescue on the beach, shortly after we ran into each other at the office," Ken proudly explains to Brian. I've never seen this side of Ken before. He's always been so modest.

"Is that so?" Brian asks, becoming annoyed and maybe a little jealous.

"Okayyy!" I say, interrupting the awkward conversation between Ken and Brian. "Ken, why don't I make you a plate—here, this one is actually ready for you." I try to hand him the full plate of food that was intended for me, but he continues to glare at Brian. "You should go ahead and sit outside," I tell Ken. "I will meet you at the table in just a couple minutes, right after I grab a plate of food for myself, okay?" I force the plate into Ken's hands and gently push him in the direction of my parents' backyard.

Once he is outside, I apologize to Brian. "Sorry, I don't know what came over him. He's usually not like that."

"What a douche bag," Brian says. I turn my head to make sure Emily didn't hear the harsh words coming from Brian's mouth. Now, I am positive he is jealous.

I'm relieved to see Emily still joyfully playing with Genesis in the living room. She hadn't heard any of our conversation.

"Your boyfriend is a real modest guy," Brian says while he finishes piling food onto his plate.

"I told you! He's not my boyfriend!" I whisper angrily.

"Fine! If he's not your boyfriend, go out with me next weekend," Brian demands. I ignore him and continue to place a spoonful of rice noodles onto my plate. "Did you hear me, Eva?" Brian purposely starts to talk more loudly, almost screaming. "If he's not your boyfriend—"

"Shhh!" I tell him. I look over my shoulder and notice Emily turn and glance at us. I yank at the sleeve of his shirt, pulling him farther away from prying ears.

"Fine. One date," I say quietly.

"Do you promise?" he asks. I guess Brian doesn't trust me. He must think I will go back on my word.

"Yes! I promise! Now be quiet!" I say, annoyed.

"What are you two lovebirds doing over here in the corner all by yourselves?" Brandi says as she pushes us both into an awkward three-way hug and kisses us both on our cheeks. I now see that she doesn't mind her brother and me talking to one another in public, completely different than our encounter during our high school days. I knew she would eventually get over the phase of being embarrassed by her little brother.

Brian and I walk outside to sit with Ken. There's a smug look on Brian's face as we start eating, produced from the thought of taking me out on a date next weekend. I'm scared that Brian is going to say something about seeing me in my lingerie, but he is completely silent throughout our entire meal.

I hold Genesis on my hip as we bid our guests goodbye.

"Happy birthday, Genesis," Emily says as she kisses my daughter's forehead. "It was so nice to meet you both. Thank you for inviting me. I had a wonderful time."

"Of course. Thank you for coming and spending time with us," I tell her.

"Hopefully, I can visit again soon, or maybe the three of you could drive to L.A. for a weekend," Emily says and gives us a warm hug.

"Yeah, that would be nice," I reply to Emily. I start to imagine all the fancy restaurants Ken would want to take me to in Los Angeles if we ended up visiting his sister.

"Goodbye, Genesis," Ken says. He kisses my cheek. "Will I see you next weekend?" Ken looks over at Brian talking to my dad. He's not sure what to think of Brian. Is he a family friend or something more?

"Uh—I..." I stumble over my words thinking back to the promise I had just made Brian. "Yeah, um, maybe. I will text you."

"I look forward to seeing you next weekend. I can cook you dinner again at my place, if you'd like," he tells me. I think of the delicious meal he had cooked for me on our second date at his mansion—unforgettable and undeniably delicious.

"Okay," I agree. "But I'm not sure if Saturday or Sunday would be best," I say, secretly referring to what would work better with Brian's schedule. "I will text you in a couple days and let you know."

Ken takes a second glance at my dad, chatting it up with Brian. "Okay, sounds good," he says as he gives me a peck on the mouth. "I'll see you next weekend."

I walk over to my dad and Brian after Emily and Ken head out the door. Genesis instantly holds her arms up and leans toward Brian. "Up, up," Genesis says, smiling at Brian.

"Wow, you must've made a good impression on her last weekend," I say, surprised. Genesis has warmed up to Brian so quickly.

"Come here, birthday girl!" he says and eagerly takes my daughter out of my arms. Genesis pats the back of Brian's shoulder with her hand and giggles.

My dad turns away from Brian and starts talking to one of my uncles, finally giving Brian a break from their conversation. "So, where should I take you next weekend for our *date*?" Brain asks, rubbing the promise I made him in my face.

"I don't know. You can decide. Isn't it the guy's job to plan the date anyway?" I say to him, jokingly.

"Wow, Eva, I didn't take you for the sexist type!" he responds, sarcastically. "All right. I will think of something," he says and then kisses Genesis on the top of her head.

What have I gotten myself into? I've never dated two guys at the same time. It feels strange and kind of wrong. Obviously, Brian doesn't mind, but I wonder how Ken would feel if he found out.

Fried Rice

After all the guests have left the party, except for Brandi, I sit down with Genesis and my parents in the living room. Brandi joins us but is texting on her phone, probably talking to Max before he starts his shift at the hospital. Presents from our generous family and friends line the fireplace. I sit on the carpet with Genesis between my legs.

"Oh, open the gift from your father and me first, Hunny," my mom says as she hands me a small box. I open it up and in there, lying in the box is a beautiful, dark green jade bracelet. It is the perfect size for Genesis' baby wrist. I gently squeeze my daughter's fingers together so I can slide the bracelet on. My parents' eyes light up, seeing their gift dangle on their granddaughter's arm.

Over the years, I have learned that it is common for mothers and grandmothers to pass down or purchase jade bracelets for their daughters and granddaughters. When my mom gifted me one of her jade bracelets on my sixteenth birthday, she explained that the bracelet was a symbol of her love for me. My mom also told me that she would always be here to protect me, for as long as she could. Even though I was on my way to becoming a young woman, my mom reminded me that I would always be her little girl.

"Thank you, Mom and Dad. It's perfect," I say as my heart fills with joy.

Brandi takes a minute away from her phone. "Mine next!" she says, getting up from the couch. She slides a huge, wrapped box in front of Genesis and me. I tear off a small piece of wrapping paper at the corner of the box and encourage Genesis to finish unwrapping the present. We laugh as she begins to aggressively rip off small fistfuls of paper, and then another, and another. I end up helping her unwrap the present because it would take all night if I let her do it by herself.

"Brandi, I told you this would take up too much room in your living room!" I say, looking at the unwrapped gift.

"I don't mind. Plus, you will need it eventually," she replies as she smiles at us. It's a stroller for Genesis.

"Thank you. I really appreciate it. *We* really appreciate it!" I say.

"This is from Auntie Joni and Uncle Alvin," my dad says. He pulls out a red envelope from his pocket and hands it to me. The small red envelope has gold Chinese symbols with peach-colored flowers in the background. I reach over and stick it in Genesis' baby bag. I don't need to open the envelope to know what's inside.

When I was younger and celebrated my birthdays,

my grandparents, aunties and uncles, and sometimes even close family friends, would give me red envelopes as a gift. When I received a red envelope on my sixth birthday, I was old enough to voice my curiosities. I asked my mom why Auntie Joanne and Uncle Dave, as well as many of our other relatives and friends, had put money into a red envelope. I wondered why they hadn't just put the money in a birthday card. My mom explained to me that, normally, these red envelopes are given to children from their relatives on Chinese New Year, but the envelopes were also given at special events. She told me the color red symbolizes good luck and happiness. Genesis and I definitely needed some happiness and extra money in our lives, that's for sure.

I notice another large box and pull it closer to Genesis and myself. It reads: *To Genesis, From Ken (and Emily)*. Genesis and I eagerly unwrap the present, maybe more so me than Genesis.

"Oh, uh, it's a dollhouse," I say.

"It looks like a French-style dollhouse," my mom corrects me. "And it looks handmade."

"Yeah, and expensive!" Brandi says. "I'm gonna look it up and see if I can find it on the internet." She holds up the phone to her face again and starts to search for the dollhouse.

171

I look at all the details inside of the dollhouse. It does look handmade like my mom had mentioned. The rooms inside the dollhouse look like they have real wallpaper lining each wall, complete with crown molding. The flooring looks like real hardwood, and there are shiny chandeliers hanging on the ceilings, as well as intricate fans and detailed light fixtures. The dark blue exterior and white shutters are hand-painted perfectly. I cannot find one flaw.

"Ah! Genesis. No!" I yell as I yank the small, handmade dining chair out of her hand. Apparently, Ken also gave Genesis a ton of tiny, porcelain accessories to help furnish the dollhouse, accessories that are much too small for a one-year-old. "I don't want you to choke on that, baby girl," I say while I tediously gather all the little pieces of furniture. My mom hands me a small cardboard box to put the pieces in.

"Oh my gosh, Eva!" Brandi says. She holds her hand over her mouth and shows me the dollhouse on her phone. She had found it on a crafting site, a site where people sell their masterpieces. It was the exact French-style dollhouse that was sitting in my parents' living room. "Only $3,500.00," Brandi says, sarcastically.

"Oh, wow, um, all right," I stutter. "Maybe you should keep this at your house until Genesis gets a little older? Maybe a lot older?" I say to my parents.

Fried Rice

"Yeah, maybe that's a good idea," my mom says, carefully lifting the dollhouse to take it into their spare bedroom. My dad chuckles quietly to himself but doesn't say anything. Such a generous gift, but a gift that wasn't really suited for a one-year-old, and we all knew it.

Next, Genesis helps me pull out different shades of pink tissue paper from a bag that has different types of animals printed all over the outside. Genesis quickly throws the rest of the tissue paper on the floor, and I pull out a soft gray elephant with large tusks and black eyes from the gift bag. Genesis grabs the stuffed animal from my hand and squeezes it tightly. She starts to jibber-jabber, in her happy baby voice.

"Oh, you like that, huh, baby girl?" I ask her. It makes me smile to see her so excited over her new stuffed animal. I reach into the bag a second time and pull out a onesie that's covered in pink ladybugs. It reads *Mommy's Little Love Bug*. "So, cute," I say to Genesis and hold it up for her to look at. She glances at it for a moment and goes back to snuggling with her stuffed elephant.

"Who's that from?" my mom asks.

"Uh, I dunno. I don't think I saw a tag," I say, double-checking the handle of the bag and looking on the outside, but nothing. I stick my hand in the bag and feel around on the bottom. "Oh, here's the card." I notice the card matches the gift bag. I open the card, and two tickets fall out onto the floor. I read the card to myself.

Genesis,

I can't believe you are already one. I hope you enjoy your special birthday. I'm glad to have been able to spend time with you and your mom last weekend. Maybe your mom and I can take you to the zoo sometime soon.

Love,
  Brian

"So, who's it from?" my mom continues to ask.

"Oh, it's from Brian," I answer, picking the zoo tickets off the floor. I try to hide my excitement from reading Brian's card, so my parents don't ask me to read it aloud. I feel like the writing in the card was meant for me.

"Ooh, Brian bought you and me tickets to the San Diego Zoo," Brandi says excitedly but also jokingly.

"What a sweet gift," my mom says.

I agree. What a thoughtful gift. The thought of taking Genesis to the zoo with Brian made me feel elated. I again thought about Ken's ridiculously expensive gift and how it wasn't practical for Genesis. I felt kind of guilty comparing Brian's gift to Ken's.

"Okay, this one is from Auntie Mae and Uncle Steve," I say, unwrapping the present. "Oh, it's a little play purse that talks. It even has a plastic credit card, so she can practice spending Mommy's money," I say, and we all chuckle together. "And there are some keys and a little mirror. So cute, Genesis look." I place the toy in front of her. "See, you can push the buttons and everything," I tell her, pulling her hand away from the stuffed elephant. She yanks her hand away from the toy and continues to hug her elephant.

"Why don't you finish opening the rest of her presents while I hold her?" my mom suggests. I pick Genesis up and set her on my mom's lap. Genesis is content and continues to snuggle her stuffed elephant.

Chapter Nineteen

For the Love of Boba

I throw on some comfy clothes—jean shorts and a loose-fitting shirt. "So, I'm going on a date with Brian today... He should be here any minute," I tell Brandi, hesitantly.

"Oh, I know," she says, without a hint of surprise in her voice. Brandi is lying down on the couch and holding Genesis up in the air like Superwoman.

"You knew? How did you know that?" I ask, surprised.

A few days ago, I asked Brandi if she could watch Genesis this next Saturday before she had to go to work, so I could go on another date. I hadn't told her it was a date with her brother and not Ken. I wasn't sure how she was going to react, so I left out that important detail until the last minute. Even though she was fine with me talking to her brother, I wasn't sure if she was going to be okay with her brother taking me out. Maybe I felt uneasy because Brandi knew I was also seeing Ken.

"Brian texted me a couple days ago, asking about you," Brandi explains.

"What did he ask about?" I say, unsure of what to expect.

"Nothing too important, just a couple questions about how serious you and Ken are and whatnot."

"What did you tell Brian?" I ask, curiously.

"Just that I know you've been on a few dates with Ken, that's all," Brandi says. "Oh, he also asked about Genesis' father."

The doorbell rings, and I answer the door. Sasuke accompanies me, happily wagging his tail. Brian is wearing a tank top, cargo shorts, and sneakers. I feel relieved that I'm not underdressed for our date. I realize that I've created a ridiculous fear from going on dates with Ken.

"Hey, beautiful," Brian says to me in front of his sister. I feel slightly uncomfortable.

"Hi… yourself?" I respond, awkwardly. "So, what do you have planned for us today?" I ask.

"Nothing fancy, but go ahead and get Genesis in her stroller. We're going to go for a walk."

"Oh, we are?" I say while grabbing my pair of running shoes that haven't been used in a very long time.

"Well, I guess Genesis is actually coming with us, Brandi," I tell her, surprised.

She just smiles like she already knew what the plan was. She is in the middle of changing Genesis and getting her ready for our walk. She puts Genesis in her new stroller, and I am thankful Brandi had bought it for her niece's birthday present. Genesis reaches for her elephant, and Brandi places the stuffed animal in my daughter's lap. I guess the elephant is going for a walk too.

"How far are we going?" I ask as I follow Brian, pushing Genesis in her stroller.

"We are almost there," he reassures me.

"My cardio is terrible," I tell him. I'm already slightly out of breath. "You're walking so fast."

"Or maybe it's because your legs are so short," Brian mocks me.

"Ha, ha, ha!" I glare at him, but he is right. My legs are short. Brian is about a foot taller than I am, and, therefore, his legs are much longer than mine. For every one step he takes, I have to take two. "Genesis seems to be enjoying her stroll," I mention.

"Yeah, I thought she would," Brian says while smiling and looking at Genesis.

Genesis is leaning over the side of her stroller, looking at the bright blue sky, and hugging her stuffed elephant tightly. She's enjoying the birds chirping. Then, Genesis quickly grabs her hearing aid and tosses it on the sidewalk. Brian abruptly stops the stroller and picks it up off the ground. He puts it into my daughter's ear with ease.

"Oh, did Brandi show you how to do that too?" I ask, shocked.

"Yeah, she did. She had me practice a few times before she and Max left the other night. She told me that Genesis takes it out sometimes. How long has she had the hearing aid?"

"Since she was about four or five months old," I answer.

"So, the doctors found out right away then?"

"Mm-hmm, they did a newborn screening at the hospital right after she was born."

"Was it hard?" Brian asks.

"Uh, yeah, I mean… I had to push for like three hours straight, and I had to get a bunch of stitches in my—"

"No, I don't mean the actual giving birth part." Brian chuckles. "I mean, was it hard to go through all of it on your own?"

I realize he's referring to Liam being absent throughout everything. I wasn't sure how much Brandi had told him either. "Yeah, it was tough. I wish I had someone by my side when Genesis was born. I mean, my mom was in the delivery room for support, and she was amazing. I don't know what I would've done without her."

"I can't believe that bastard left you while you were four months pregnant with Genesis." Apparently, Brandi had told him quite a bit.

"Yeah, it sucked, but we are figuring it out on our own, aren't we, pretty lady?" I say to Genesis, leaning toward her as we walk.

"We're here. See, I told you it wasn't much farther," Brian says. I had forgotten about my poor cardio while talking to Brian. I really enjoyed his company.

"Aw, you brought me to my favorite local tea spot." I smile at him and give him a hug. "Thank you! I'm assuming Brandi also told you about my love of boba."

He nods. "Yeah, I asked her if I should take you out to get coffee, but she told me that getting coffee on a first date is super cliché and that you hate coffee but love boba. Good thing I asked, huh?"

"Yeah, good thing." I laugh.

I order a matcha milk tea with boba, and Brian orders a Vietnamese coffee. We sit down at the table outside.

"Do you want some, Genesis?" he asks her while putting the straw up to her mouth. She tries to grab the cup out of his hand.

"She can't have that!" I say, shoving his shoulder with my closed fist.

"I know." He chuckles and pulls the cup away from Genesis. "I was only kidding."

I pull out her sippy cup of water from her diaper bag and hand it to her. The three of us enjoy our drinks. "So, what did you want to do after this?" Brian asks me.

I feel butterfly wings graze the inside of my stomach as I become elated at the thought of spending more time with Brian. I try to play down my excitement and say, "I don't know. I mean, I kept my promise. I'm sitting here, on a date with you."

"Yeah, okay, true, true," he says and smiles. "But I would really like to spend more time with you tonight if you aren't busy."

I shrug, still suppressing my true emotions. "I don't have any plans. So, I guess we can hang out, but just because you brought me to my favorite tea place," I tell him.

Brian smirks, satisfied with my answer. "Should we just stay in, and I'll order pizza? We can hang out at your place with Genesis, and we can watch another movie. I will let Genesis pick the movie again. She picks the best ones." He makes me laugh. "You know, then we can just have a relaxing night in tonight."

"Yeah, that actually sounds pretty great," I tell him. He reaches over to hold my hand while we finish our drinks, and the butterflies return.

"Oh, the pizza's here," I say as I go to grab my wallet.

"I'll get it, Eva," Brian insists. He pays the delivery guy and walks to the kitchen to plate the pizza.

"Come on, Genesis. Brian bought us dinner," I say to her and place her in her highchair.

Brian puts a couple slices of pizza on each of our plates. "So, do you want me to chop up some for Genesis too?" Brian asks, not sure if Genesis is capable of chewing through the crunchy crust with her eight front teeth. "I don't remember feeding Carly pizza."

"Yeah, this girl loves to eat anything and everything, just like her mama, huh Genesis? You just have to make sure the pieces are small enough for her to chew but not choke on," I tell Brian.

Genesis screams while banging on her tray attached to her highchair, demanding dinner as soon as possible. I scoot her into the living room so we can finish watching *The Little Mermaid* together.

Watching *The Little Mermaid* makes me think of Ken, and I start to feel guilty hanging out with Brian. I try to justify the promise I made Brian at Genesis' birthday party—Ken and I aren't exclusively dating. For all I know, Ken could be dating three other women. Right this very moment, he could be dining at an expensive restaurant with some blonde bombshell. I knew none of this was true.

"What are you thinking about?" Brian asks me as he puts baby-sized pieces of pizza onto Genesis' tray.

"Mmm!" she says and then shoves the food into her mouth.

"Uh—nothing," I lie.

"What are you thinking about?" I ask Brian.

"Just that I love spending time with you and Genesis, and how Liam is missing out on you two wonderful girls," Brian replies.

He makes me blush. "We love spending time with you too. Isn't that right, Genesis?" She looks at me and then at Brian and giggles. Pizza sauce covers the corners of her mouth, and she smiles her cute toothy smile.

Brian brings us our plates of pizza, and I notice there are olives on top of my slices. I start to pick the nasty little rings off and set them on the edge of my plate.

"Oh, I didn't know you don't like olives," Brian says.

"It's fine. I don't mind taking them off," I tell him. "It's my fault for telling you to surprise me when you asked what kind of pizza I wanted."

"Ah, you should've said something," he says, disappointed.

"It's really not a big deal. I usually will eat anything and everything, like I was saying, but there's just something about olives. They are really gross." I look over at Brian, and he looks bummed. "Thank you for buying us dinner. I really appreciate it," I say and push the pile of my olives I've collected onto Genesis' tray. "See, they aren't going to waste. Genesis is happy." She aggressively grabs the entire mound of olives I set in front of her and happily shoves them into her mouth.

Brian laughs. "All right. Well, I'm glad Genesis is enjoying the olives."

Once again, Genesis begins to get sleepy a few minutes before the movie is over. I have déjà vu as I watch Brian change Genesis into a fresh diaper, dress her in her pajamas, feed her a bottle, and tuck her into bed. He gently pulls out her hearing aid and puts it in the case.

"See, Eva, I remembered this time." He's proud that he remembered to take out her hearing aid, and so am I.

"How many kids do you want to have?" I ask Brian, thinking back to the conversation I had with Ken on our third date.

"Whoa! Whoa! It's only our first date, Eva. Don't

get ahead of yourself," he says.

I'm falling in love with Brian's sense of humor, and I can't help but chuckle at his joke. "Seriously, though, how many?" I ask. "I want to know."

He doesn't need any extra time to think about his response. "At least one would be nice, but really, however many my future wife wants. If she wants one, that's fine, but if she wants six, I'm down," he says.

"Wow, six is a lot of kids," I say. "You'd probably be working a lot of overtime," I joke.

He shrugs. "Yeah, I guess. I wouldn't mind. What about you? Are you happy with just one?"

"I've thought about it a little, but it's not like I have anyone to make babies with at the moment, anyway." I laugh but then start to think about Genesis not having a sister or brother to grow up with. It saddens me. I know the feeling of being a single child. "I think it would be nice to give Genesis a brother or sister to grow up with. My parents didn't give me that opportunity, you know, to have the kind of bond you and Brandi share. But, yeah, I don't know about having more than two kids. I feel like the attention I would be able to provide for all the kids would be spread too thin."

He nods. "Yeah, I understand where you are coming from, but I agree, I'm pretty lucky to have Brandi as an older sister. She's pretty great."

185

*****

We stand at the front door to say our goodbyes. "Well, promise fulfilled," I say, gazing into his eyes.

"Yeah, about that… I know our promise only entailed one date, but"—Brian continues—"I want to ask you if I can take you and Genesis to the zoo tomorrow? I think she would have a lot of fun, and we can use those tickets I got for Genesis."

I smirk at Brian. "Oh, I thought those tickets were for Genesis and me," I say, jokingly.

"Genesis gets in for free," Brian says, trying to counter my joke.

"I mean, I thought those tickets were for Brandi and me to take Genesis to the zoo," I say, still joking around.

Then I remember I'm supposed to go over to Ken's for dinner tomorrow night since I didn't go over today, but I really want to see Brian again, and he did buy us those tickets to the zoo.

"Yeah, that works for me," I say, feeling kind of terrible for ignoring Ken's date night request.

My heart begins to race, anticipating what's to come next. Brian places his hands around my waist and pulls me in close to his body. He places his mouth on mine. My hands reach up to touch the back of his neck, and I am lost. I'm lost in his strong but tender embrace and soft lips. Brian continues to kiss me, long and hard. I don't want it to end, but he eventually pulls away. He keeps his forehead pressed up against mine, and we look into each other's eyes for a moment. My hands are still on his neck, and his hands still caress my waist.

"Bye," he says.

"Bye," I say, wishing I could replay our day over again.

"I will see you tomorrow," he says and walks out the door. I nod, satisfied with my goodbye kiss.

Chapter Twenty

Snakes are my Favorite

"What animals do you want to see first?" I ask Brian as we walk up to the zoo's entrance. A statue of a lion stands as high as a two-story building. The golden lion looks as if he had just landed from jumping into the air. His front paws are placed on the ground, but his back legs have been thrust upward from his gigantic leap. Genesis points to the statue and says something in her excited baby talk.

"Whatever you girls want to see, but first, I want to take you to lunch if you are hungry. If not, we can wait until a little later," Brian tells me.

"I would love some lunch, and I'm sure Genesis would too," I say as I intertwine my arm around Brian's.

I slyly slide my hand onto Brian's hard bicep as he pushes Genesis in her stroller. He smirks, and I feel him try to flex his bicep.

188

Fried Rice

*****

We sit down for lunch in the outside seating area. I can hear water splashing onto rocks, and so does Genesis. She points to the waterfall that's surrounded by tropical plants and begins kicking her little legs against her highchair out of excitement.

"She really likes the waterfall," Brian says, happy with his restaurant choice.

"Yeah, she does. She's so excited," I say.

"What are you going to order?" Brian asks.

"I was thinking of getting the mushroom risotto with shrimp," I say.

"Oh, fancy," he responds.

"What about you? What are you going to have?" I ask him.

"I'm just going to get the burger and fries," he says. "Then I can share my fries with Genesis. Every kid likes fries, right Genesis?" They cutely smile at one another.

This was nice—just a casual lunch date with my darling Genesis and handsome date.

The server brings us our food. "Oh wow, this risotto is so good," I say, helping myself to another bite.

"Yeah, the food is always good here."

"Have you eaten at this restaurant before?" I ask.

"Yeah, I've been here a couple of times with Clarissa," he says. He winces from bringing up his ex-girlfriend.

"Oh, Clarissa from high school?" I ask, not fazed by his answer.

Clarissa was a girl in the same grade as Brian. I remembered seeing them walk down the halls together during the middle of his freshman year. I also recall going over to hang out at Brandi's house and seeing Brian and Clarissa making out on the couch.

"Yeah," he says. "Sorry, I didn't mean to bring that up," he apologizes, worried that he might've brought up a poor subject to talk about.

"It's fine, Brian. High school was a long time ago," I reassure him. "When did you guys break up?"

He nervously rubs his neck. "Uh, well, I broke up with her the day after... I babysat Genesis." Brian winces.

I am in complete and utter shock. The day after he babysat Genesis? That was like, a week ago, to be exact. "Oh, so you guys have only been broken up for about a week then?" I say, trying to subtly play down my panic.

"Yeah, I meant to tell you, but it was hard for me to find the right time," he says. Brian looks nervous, but I'm really not all that mad. Wait, am I mad? I don't know. How could I be? I'm dating Ken and Brian at the same time, but I don't think I can compare my relationships to his and Clarissa's. It's not the same. They were together for an extremely long time.

"Wait, am I the reason you guys broke up?" I ask Brian.

"Um, no and yes," he answers. *Oh, please, please let this conversation go smoothly*, I think to myself. Brian continues, "The last few months, I could feel us slowly drifting apart. I thought we were on the same page, but apparently, she has different goals for her future. That's actually why I purchased my condo, under my name. I wasn't fully confident our relationship was going to last and decided to move out on my own."

"Oh, okay. So, you were planning on breaking up with her anyway?" I ask, hopeful Brian doesn't tell me something I don't want to hear.

"Uh, I wasn't sure I should break up with her, but then I realized I had legitimate feelings for you," Brian explains.

Okay. I think I'm good with that answer. I'm not mad. "Oh, okay. That's understandable. Uh, so, how did she take it? Did you tell her about me?" I ask, anxiously.

"Um, I kind of left you out of it. I didn't want to hurt her feelings any more than I had to."

"That's nice of you. Probably a good idea you didn't say anything."

"Yeah, I just told her that I felt like we were growing apart, and I thought it would be best if we broke up," he tells me. He's giving me such vague answers, but

I'm not sure that I want to know any more details. I'm worried I won't be able to look past their real reasons for breaking up.

"Ugh, breakups are the worst," I say. "Is she doing okay?" I ask, sincerely concerned for Clarissa as I think back to the day Liam had left me.

"I don't know," Brian says. "She's been ignoring me since the breakup."

I was kind of happy to hear she wasn't talking to him. I'm not sure how it would be with his ex in the picture. "How are you doing? Do you miss her?" I ask, hesitantly.

"I mean, it was a big change not seeing her every day, but I know it isn't right for me to stay in a relationship that's wrong for me, especially if I have feelings for you."

I kind of feel like a homewrecker. Am I a homewrecker? "I will just have to trust your word, I suppose," I say and try to sort out my feelings.

He stands up from his seat and slowly walks around Genesis' highchair. Brian squats down next to my chair. I look down at him, confused and silent. He looks me directly in the eyes, places his hand on my thigh, and says, "I really do have strong feelings for you. I'm so thankful you let me take you out yesterday and today." Brian grabs the back of my head and kisses me in front of all the diners, including their children.

I hear one lady say, "Okay, that's enough!" Another person whistles and begins to hoot and holler at our public display of affection. Genesis is clapping her hands.

"Do you forgive me for not telling you about Clarissa sooner?" he asks me, looking into my eyes again.

"Yes, I forgive you." I give him one last peck before he returns to his seat.

I forgive him, but I can't help that I still feel a little insecure about his previous relationship. I hope it won't interfere with Brian's and my relationship.

"Okay, ladies, where to first?" Brian asks us as he pushes Genesis in her stroller. "What's your favorite animal to see at the zoo?" he asks me.

"Well, the snakes are my favorite," I tell him.

"Okay, perfect. The reptile enclosures are toward the front. We can start there and work our way around," he suggests.

"Sounds good," I say, excited to start our zoo adventure.

"Oh, wow. Come look at this humongous snake, Eva." Brian is pointing at the albino python slithering through its enclosure as it senses its surroundings with its tongue.

"For a second, I thought you were going to show me the humongous snake in your pants."

He acknowledges my lame joke. "Maybe another day," he says.

"Do you promise?" I ask, jokingly, not expecting an answer. I look at the sixteen-foot snake. "Wow. He's really awesome. He has the most interesting yellow and white patterns."

"Would you ever get one of these as a pet, but like a smaller ball python?" Brian asks me.

"Yeah, maybe when Genesis gets older. I guess it's probably highly unlikely that it would choke her out, but I would still be paranoid."

"You could take him, huh Genesis?" Brian asks her while laughing. He bends over and squeezes Genesis' chubby baby arm between his index finger and thumb. "Look at these thick baby guns. No way the snake would stand a chance.

I point to an enclosure filled with colorful corn snakes. "Look at these, Brian. Their colors are so vibrant, and it's neat how they look kind of slimy, but they really aren't."

Brian wraps his arm around my shoulder and pulls me close to the side of his body. He kisses the top of my head. "You are so weird, but I love it. Come on, let's go see the orangutans. I heard there's a baby."

There is a darling little baby orangutan clenching tightly on to its mama's back, but I'm more interested in the one sitting farther away in the enclosure.

"Brian, the orangutan with reddish hair is eating her own poop!" I point to the orangutan that's shoveling her own dung into her mouth. The large orangutan is sitting in the dirt beside two boulders. She is really going to town and enjoying her feast.

Brian walks over to me with Genesis on his shoulders. He had taken her out of her stroller, so she could get a better look. Now, she can get a better look at this orangutan devouring her own feces!

"Oh"—he starts to laugh—"yeah. I think they eat their poop to get a second round of nutrients they can't digest the first time."

I wince as I watch the orangutan continue to consume its poop. For whatever reason, it's hard for me to avert my gaze. It's kind of like that time Brandi was watching some nasty medical procedure on TV. Even though I kept telling her to change it to something else, I continued to watch the entire show. "I seriously think I have a legit fear of poop," I tell Brian. He laughs as he buckles Genesis back into her stroller.

Next, we walk over to see the elephants, and Brian sits Genesis on the wooden rail that helps barricade off the enclosure. He tries to get Genesis to look at the baby elephant playing in the water. She eventually spots the jubilant elephant splashing water onto its back with its trunk, and she starts to smile and giggle. She is having a blast at the zoo, and so is Brian.

I sit down on one of the wooden benches that overlooks the elephant enclosure. I pull out my phone and notice I had a text from Ken: *"Hey, Eva, I was wondering if I was going to be able to see you tonight? I haven't heard from you all week, and I was wondering if you were still free?"*

Ken was right—he hadn't heard from me all week, and I hadn't made it a priority to text him, not once. I respond to his text: *"I'm sorry, I meant to text you, but got busy. I won't be able to make it over tonight, but I can come over next weekend on Saturday. I promise."* Oops, another promise.

He quickly texts me back: *"Okay, I miss you. I will hold you to it."*

I feel pressured to keep all my promises. I should probably stop making so many.

"Who's that?" Brian asks, buckling Genesis into her stroller.

"Oh, no one," I lie. I stick the phone back into my

pocket. "You about ready to head out?" I ask.

"Yeah, I think Genesis is getting a little sleepy. Do you want to go back to your place, and I can order us another pizza for dinner?" Brian asks.

"Sure, that sounds nice," I tell him.

We walk in front of the gift shops on our way toward the exit. Genesis starts whining and reaches for a stuffed elephant in one of the outside displays.

"No, Genesis. You already have one at home. You don't need another one, pretty girl," I say, but Brian stops pushing the stroller to look at the stuffed elephant.

"It looks a little different than the one I got her for her birthday," he says, but I'm pretty confident they look almost the same. I look at it more closely and notice the one in the display looks more like a baby elephant with no tusks, and it's slightly smaller. He picks up the elephant and hands it to Genesis. He pulls out his wallet to pay the cashier.

"How much is it?" he asks the salesgirl, who is dressed in a safari uniform.

"Brian, you don't have to do that," I say. "You already got her one for her birthday."

"I want to. Look how happy she is," he says.

Genesis is really happy. She's hugging the elephant tightly just like she did with the one at her birthday party.

"Now Genesis has a daddy elephant and a baby elephant. Just what every girl needs," Brian says. He warms my heart with his sweet words.

"Did you want to purchase a second one? They are one for $10.00 or two for $15.00," the salesgirl tells Brian.

"All right. I will go ahead and take a snake too," he says.

I can't help but smile when Brian dangles the stuffed snake around the back of my neck. I take a minute to admire the pink sequins. "Oh, the scales change color when you pet the snake," I say as I show Brian. I giggle and stroke my pet snake, turning the "scaly skin" over with my fingers. "It was pink, and now it's black!" I say, smiling at him.

"I'm glad you like it," he says.

"I do. I love it. Thank you." I kiss him again as we exit the park.

"So, does this mean that I get to take you on another date next weekend?"

"I don't know, maybe?" I say. "What did you have in mind?"

"Have you been to the aquarium lately?" he asks me.

"No, but I would love to go with you next weekend," I say, excitedly.

"How does Saturday sound?" he asks.

Oh no, I think to myself, remembering my most recent promise to Ken. "Um, could we do Sunday instead?" I ask, hopeful.

"I actually have to attend a training class all day Sunday for work. It's mandatory," he explains.

"What time does the aquarium open?" I ask, hoping it opens fairly early.

"I think it opens at 11:00 a.m.," he tells me.

"All right. I think Saturday will work out, as long as we arrive when it opens and leave before 4:00."

We arrive home, and Brian places the pizza order over the phone.

"Genesis picked *Tangled*," Brian says from the living room.

"That's one of my favorites," I tell him.

I'm in the kitchen making a salad as an appetizer for us to eat before the pizza arrives. Brian puts Genesis on the floor in the living room. She starts to crawl around the room, finds her way to the couch, and bravely pulls herself up.

"Oh, look, Eva!" Brian says as he points to Genesis standing beside the couch.

I smile. "She's been doing that every now and then." We continue to watch Genesis stand while she holds on to the couch. Then, she lifts her arms up and practices balancing on her own two feet for the very first time. She wobbles slightly, swaying back and forth, attempting to keep her balance. "Oh my gosh, Genesis! Good job, baby girl!" I start to clap my hands, encouraging her to stand without support for a while longer, but she quickly falls onto her bottom. "That was the first time she stood all by herself," I tell Brian.

"Great job, Genesis! You are such a strong lady," Brian says to her. He notices that I am done in the kitchen, and he puts Genesis back into her bouncer.

"Here's your salad. I made sesame dressing," I tell him.

He takes a bite. "This is really good," he says. He nods his head multiple times and continues to eat his salad.

"You made this dressing from scratch?" he asks.

"Yeah, one of my mom's family recipes," I tell him.

"Oh, you know what? This reminds me of that one time I went over to your parents' house with Brandi. That one time your parents wanted to meet me," he says.

"Yeah, they really wanted to have you over for dinner. They just had to meet Brandi's little brother. My parents are funny like that," I say.

"Yeah, Brandi was so mad. She didn't want me going over to your parents' for dinner. She was so embarrassed by me back then." We start to laugh as we reminiscence about the past. "I actually think your mom made us Chinese chicken salad for dinner that night if I remember correctly. Is this the same dressing?"

"Yeah, it is—the exact same one. You have a good memory," I tell him, feeling smug with my choice of dressing.

"Oh man, that salad was so good. The dressing was dynamite. I couldn't forget it, even if I tried. I probably ate five bowls that evening," he says.

"Yeah, you really got on my mom's good side with those professional eating skills of yours," I say as we both laugh.

"Man, Eva. That's when I really started crushing on you hard," he says. I feel my face become warm from Brian's blunt flattery.

Sasuke jumps out of his bed and runs to the door to protect us from the delivery guy. "Let me get it this time. You already treated us to lunch."

"All right, if you insist," he says.

When I open the box, I see that Brian hadn't ordered any olives. He remembered.

This was when I learned *food is a form of selflessness.*

"You didn't get any olives on the pizza this time," I state.

201

"You picked them off last time," he responds.

"You could've just gotten half of the pizza without olives."

"I could've, but what if you wanted to eat more than half the pizza?" he half-jokes.

"Ha, ha!" I say as I give him a dirty look. I plate our pizza and begin to chop up some for Genesis. "Well, I appreciate the selfless thought."

Chapter Twenty-One

Double Date

I stare at Brian holding Genesis. We are standing in the dimly lit aquarium. The dark brown flooring reminds me of being on a wooden ship. Brightly colored fish swim all around us, accompanied by leopard sharks, which are almost as long as I am. There is a separate tank that's lit up by purple lights—home to a dozen clear jellyfish. Brian takes Genesis over to the large cylinder tank that is filled with sea jellies. Genesis tries to touch them through the glass, and it's such a mesmerizing sight.

"What do you think, Genesis?" I say as I walk closer to her and Brian. She's still staring at the jellyfish elegantly swimming in the water. "This is really amazing, Brian. Thank you for taking us out again," I tell him.

Brian has a smirk on his face. "No problem. I'm glad I was able to persuade you to spend more time with me," he responds.

I look at the time on my phone. "Shit," I say quietly to myself, but Brian still hears me.

We had arrived at the aquarium a little later than I had hoped because Genesis had a blowout in her car seat. Right as I was almost done buckling her in, she decided to poop herself—the same thing that happened at her audiologist appointment. It took us almost an extra hour to clean her up.

"What's going on?" he asks.

"Oh, it's nothing," I shake my head. I knew I was going to be late for my date with Ken. I text Ken to see if we could meet at my parents an hour later than we had originally planned.

"Are you still seeing Ken?" Brian asks, sharply.

Ugh, I didn't want to tell him, but I didn't want to lie either. "Um, yeah. Just casually," I say, trying not to make it a big deal, but Brian looks really upset.

"Do you have something planned with him later tonight?" he asks.

Ugh! I didn't want to have to tell him about my plans this evening either! "Yeah... we are just hanging out at his place," I say, leaving out all the romantic details.

Brian doesn't respond for a while. We stand in awkward silence, looking at the fish swim by. "Well, I better get you home, so you can go on your next date,"

Brian says, irritably.

We walk back to the truck in silence, and Brian buckles Genesis into her car seat. As we get into his truck, he doesn't look as upset, but I can tell something is still bothering him. "I'm sorry, Brian," I say. "I didn't mean to upset you. I shouldn't have—"

He cuts me off. "No, you shouldn't be apologizing. I'm the one who should be saying sorry." Brian turns on the ignition but leaves his truck in park. He stares out the front window while he talks. "I made you promise to go on a date with me, knowing you were seeing someone else. It's my fault. I just"—he thinks for a moment—"I just... Ever since my first day of high school, I've had a huge crush on you. When I was just a lost freshman standing alone in the hallway, you showed me kindness. Not to mention, I thought you were the most attractive girl I'd seen that day. Then, when your parents had invited me over for dinner, I knew I really liked you but couldn't pursue you because Brandi would have never allowed it at that time. I really didn't think I was going to actually fall for you after just a couple of dates. I didn't think I would become so attached to you and Genesis in such a short amount of time."

I think my jaw is on the bottom of Brian's truck, sitting on his floor mat somewhere by my feet. I was expecting to get lectured like Liam used to lecture me when I messed up. "I—I, don't know what to say," I stammer.

He begins to pull out of the parking spot. "You don't need to say anything, Eva. I'm glad we could spend the afternoon together. It was a lot of fun."

It's quiet during the drive home.

When we arrive at the townhome, I jump out of Brian's truck and awkwardly ask him to hold Genesis for a minute while I transfer her car seat into my car. Brian puts his truck in park and gets out without saying a word. He takes Genesis from my hands and impatiently holds her. I move her car seat from his truck to my car, and I quickly toss the diaper bag and stroller into the trunk.

I take Genesis out of his arms. "Thank you for helping me," I tell him. His lips are pursed, and he looks mad, but I can also tell that I may have crushed his heart. He still doesn't say anything. I'm not really sure how I should react. "Have a goodnight," I say as he climbs into his truck. He doesn't acknowledge me and drives away. I probably wouldn't have felt as terrible as I do now if Brian had yelled at me during the car ride. I might not have felt bad at all if Brian had scolded me like Liam used to, but he didn't, and I feel like a horrible person.

I rush over to my parents' house in hopes that Ken

isn't waiting for me. He never responded to my text. He could've been hanging out at my parents' for the last hour. I think of the millions of questions they could've asked him in the last sixty minutes, prying into his life. I think of all the humiliating stories from my childhood they could've shared.

I pull up to my parents' house and see that Ken's Porsche is parked out front. "Oh, great." I unbuckle Genesis, grab her diaper bag, and sprint into my mom and dad's house.

"Ah, there she is," Ken says. He looks relieved that I'm finally here. Now I really wonder what they've been talking about.

"I am so, so sorry, Ken," I try to explain. "I lost track of time and—"
"It's no problem at all," he says. He stands up from the couch and stares at my outfit. "Uh, do you need to change… or are you ready to go?"

I had forgotten what I'd been wearing in the process of rushing over to meet up with Ken. I am dressed in jeans and a tank top. A nice outfit for the aquarium but not so nice for dinner with Ken. I look at his outfit. He's wearing a long-sleeved button-up shirt with his normal slacks and dress shoes. No surprise there. I don't think I've seen him in anything else besides on the day I got knocked out at the beach.

"I—uh, um," I stutter as my parents sit on the couch staring at me. "No, I'm ready to go." Now I am officially underdressed for my date night with Ken.

Ken looks disappointed. "I guess we will be on our way then. It was nice chatting with you Mr. and Mrs. Gin." They both stand up to hug Ken goodbye. My dad calls him Son again, and I roll my eyes. I hand Genesis to my mom, and I kiss my daughter on her cheek.

As I walk into Ken's backyard, I notice the lights are still strung up from our last romantic dinner. His backyard still looks like a five-star resort, and I sit down at the beautifully set table, underdressed and not prepared.

Ken brings out our plates of food, and once again, the meal looks exquisite and delightful.

"So, Eva, would you like to tell me who that guy was at Genesis' party last weekend? The guy you were talking to the entire time at the party? Emily and I agree you guys were acting a little strange when you two were getting your plates of food," he says, aggressively.

Wow, I guess we're getting right to the point tonight. "That... was actually, Brandi's brother," I explain while cutting into my perfectly cooked chicken cordon bleu. I wonder if his jealousy stems from his insecurities from his previous relationship.

"You guys seemed to get along pretty well," he states.

"Yeah, well, we've known each other for a while. I've known him as long as I've known Brandi," I explain.

"I see. Have you guys ever dated?" he asks, suspiciously.

Uh-oh. Seriously, how did I get myself in this situation? "Um, we went on a couple dates," I say, leaving out the details of when and where.

"Do you have feelings for him?" he asks.

What the hell? Are we playing twenty questions? Ken still hasn't taken one bite off his plate, and he has the most intense look on his face like he's struggling to open the lid on a pickle jar.

"Listen"—I try to make him understand—"I didn't think you and I were exclusively dating, so I didn't think there would be a problem with me seeing—"

"I'm not seeing anyone else, and I was hopeful you weren't either," he says sharply.

I feel like I'm being attacked. I pause from eating and lean back in my chair. I look at Ken unhappily. He realizes that I am upset, and I'm thankful to see the tension on his face disappear.

"I only want to spend time with you." He grabs my hand and kisses the top of it.

Oh, shoot. I don't know if I feel the same way he

does. I slowly pull my hand away from his and look down at my plate. "You know, Ken… you have cooked me a lot of really nice dinners, and you have taken me to some really fantastic restaurants, but I don't—"

The tension on his face starts to build again. "You don't what?" he says, trying to hide his frustration.

"I'm just not sure this is going to work out between us. I feel like I'm not really meeting your expectations," I say, pointing to the outfit I'm currently wearing. "I feel a lot of pressure having to pick the right person for me *and* Genesis."

I instantly think back to the time when I called his ex-girlfriend a bitch for cheating on him. Not that I think cheating is ever an excuse, but I start to wonder if she felt the same way I was feeling at this precise moment. I felt like I had to constantly meet his expectations. I was constantly having to walk on eggshells.

"Wait, you don't think I'm the right person for you and Genesis?" Ken asks, surprised at my comment. He forcefully places the bottom of his fists against the edge of the table, unable to subdue his emotions.

"My parents probably think you are the perfect guy for me, but we haven't spent any time together with my daughter."

"I just thought we could get to know each other better without interruptions," he tries to explain.

I start to become upset, "If you want to get to know me better, then you should get to know my daughter too. She is my whole life. Everything I do is for her. She is and always will be my first priority. I know it was my idea to drop Genesis off at my parents' during our first date, but the only time you ever held my daughter was at the beach. I wish you would've suggested taking me *and* my daughter out at least once or twice." I say, sternly.

Ken thinks for a moment and responds, "I apologize. You are right. I should've thought about how important Genesis is to you, and as for your outfit... I regret making you feel underdressed. You still look absolutely stunning in your ripped jeans and tank top."

A smile forms on my face. We are both well aware that I do not look absolutely stunning—*clearly* an exaggeration. The looming tension finally dissipates. We laugh at Ken's compliment about my outfit, and we finally start to enjoy our meal.

As I take another bite, I begin to think back to the dates I've had with Brian. Brian always wanted to spend time with me but never left my daughter out of the picture. I think back to how he treated Genesis like she was his own child, holding her on the railing to get a better view of the baby elephant. I think back to the time when he chopped up pizza into tiny pieces so Genesis wouldn't choke. I think back to how Brian lovingly laid my daughter down in her crib.

After we finish eating dinner, Ken drives me to my parents' to pick up Genesis. Instead of saying goodbye at the front door like last time, he goes inside to help me with my daughter. Genesis is asleep in my mother's arms. Before I can take Genesis from my mom, Ken picks up my sleeping baby. We say goodnight to my parents, and Ken walks us to my car. I realize that our talk this evening has done a lot of good, and Ken has actually listened to my concerns about our relationship, unlike Liam used to do. He carefully buckles Genesis into her car seat trying not to wake her. Then he gently closes the door and turns toward me to say goodnight. I assume that he is just going to give me a short kiss goodbye, but he doesn't. He kisses me for a long time. He hugs me tightly and presses my back against the side of my car. His body is touching mine. It's nice.

"Goodbye, Eva. I hope to see you next weekend. I mean, I hope to see you *and* Genesis next weekend. Will you text me?"

"Yeah, of course," I say and slide into my car. He waves as I drive away.

Ken's goodbye kiss was a lot longer this time. He even placed his body close to mine, and it was nice. It was *just* nice and nothing more.

Chapter Twenty-Two

Awkward Sisterly Questions

"How was dinner last night with Ken?" Brandi asks as she heats up fried rice for her and Genesis to share.

"It was okay," I respond.

"Just okay?" Brandi asks.

"Yeah, we actually got into a little bit of a fight," I tell her.

"You did? I'm sorry to hear that, Eva. Did you guys work everything out?"

I shrug. "I guess. Kind of."

"What happened?" Brandi asks, concerned.

"Well, I made the mistake of scheduling two dates yesterday. One with your brother in the afternoon and one with Ken at night."

"Uh-oh. It didn't go as smoothly as you had hoped?" Brandi asks.

"No, not at all. We stayed too long at the aquarium,

213

and I ended up hurting both of my dates' feelings. Then, I got into this big argument with Ken. I told Ken how I always feel the need to be plastered into some fancy dress or outfit for him and that he has never asked to spend time with Genesis. I didn't mention this to Ken, but I don't know if I should be feeling more of something. When he kisses me, it's just a kiss. Does that make any sense?"

Brandi sits down next to me at the dining room table and rubs my arm, trying to comfort me. "Yeah, you just aren't seeing fireworks when you guys kiss. It's perfectly normal to want something more. I understand, girl. That sounds tough, but maybe there's someone else out there. *Someone* else who will kiss you, and it will be more than just a kiss."

"Yeah, maybe, but my parents love Ken. If I break up with him, I'm going to disappoint my parents too."

"Your parents aren't the ones dating Ken, and you know what's best for you and Genesis. No one else does," she says. "You know, you didn't completely ruin it with my brother," Brandi tells me. She fails at hiding her smirk.

I look at her confused, and then I realize Brian had probably texted her after our date at the aquarium. "Oh, did Brian text you last night?" I ask.

She nods her head. "He did, and he's worried *he*

might've ruined things between the two of you... and Genesis." She gets up and retrieves the bowl of fried rice from the microwave. "You should talk to him," she says, encouraging me.

"I don't know. What would I say? Sorry, I'm still seeing Ken. Do you want to go on another date with me?" I say, sarcastically.

"I know you will figure it out, Eva. You always do," Brandi reassures me.

I blankly stare at my phone. What should I say to Brian? What do I say to Ken? I lower my forehead down onto the table, between my elbows and cross my arms over my head. "I don't know what to do!"

I hear Genesis giggle, and I turn my head toward her. I see Brandi playing with her niece. Before she spoons some fried rice onto her tray, she says, "You want some of this? Huh, pretty girl?" Brandi gently taps Genesis' nose with the end of the spoon. They are both giggling and smiling at one another. I cherish these moments.

Brandi finally quits teasing Genesis and puts some fried rice onto her tray. "You know, Brian really loves Genesis. He wouldn't stop talking about her after he came over to babysit her," Brandi tells me.

This makes me smile. I think back to the first night Brian watched Genesis, and he informed me that he and my daughter had eaten all the fried rice together. I think of Brian sharing his French fries with Genesis at the zoo. My heart is content as memories of Brian and my daughter flow through my mind. I realize that Ken is Mr. Right for Mr. and Mrs. Gin, but Brian is Mr. Right for Genesis and me.

"I'm going to call it off with Ken," I tell Brandi, confident in my choice. She smiles as if I had made the right decision, but she doesn't say anything. She just keeps playing with Genesis as they enjoy the fried rice together.

The next morning, I text Ken: *"I want to talk to you about something this weekend. Would it be okay if I stopped by on Saturday for a few minutes?"*

He quickly responds: *"Yes, I should be home all day. Is everything okay?"*

I don't fully answer his question and reply: *"I just think we need to talk. I will stop by around noon."*

Saturday arrives, and I drive over to Ken's place. I am nervous. Before I drove over, I couldn't decide if I should wear a nice dress or just my normal pair of jeans. I realized I was being ridiculous and opted for my ordinary pair of jeans and T-shirt.

As I pull into his driveway, I stare at his mansion one last time. I go to knock on Ken's door, but he opens it before I get the chance to. He must've been impatiently waiting for me.

"Hi, Eva, come on in. We can take a seat on the couch," he says as he directs me to his luxurious living room filled with rare art pieces. There's a statue of a man's head sitting on a tall pedestal. The expression on his marble face looks like he is about to witness something humorous.

"So, what did you want to talk about?" he asks.

I change my focus from the odd sculpture to Ken. I inhale deeply and slowly release the air out of my lungs. "Well, I wanted to come over to tell you that I don't think we should see each other anymore," I say sadly but composed in my decision.

"Is this because of our argument last week? I thought we had talked things out?" he says. Ken looks panicked.

"Uh, I mean, we did... kind of talk things out, but—"

"I told you I wanted to spend more time with Genesis and that you didn't have to get all dressed up for me anymore. What else do you want me to do?" he questions, defensively.

"It's not that I want you to change anything. I just—"

"Oh... I see. You have feelings for Brandi's

brother," he says. He loses his perfect posture as he slumps over in defeat.

I shoot him a sympathetic smile. "I do have strong feelings for Brian," I explain. "I'm sorry. It doesn't feel right to keep leading you on."

"No, I understand. I appreciate your honesty," he says. "I guess there's nothing I can do to change how you feel?"

I shake my head. "No, I just think it's for the best, but I know that one day you are going to make some girl really happy. I'm just not that girl."

Even after getting dumped, Ken still walks me to my car. I'm pretty sure he's trying not to cry in front of me. I feel horrible. I try to give him a sympathy hug, but he doesn't seem all that interested. He quickly scurries back to his mansion and doesn't wait for me to drive away.

Later that afternoon, I decided to text Brian: *"Hey Brian, I was wondering if you would want to come over tomorrow night? I would really like to cook you dinner."*

I had to wait a whole thirty minutes for a response. I sat on the couch, checking my phone every sixty seconds. Thirty minutes felt like three hours. *"Sure, but only if Genesis picks the movie."* I was surprised at his response, even with Brandi's boost of confidence. I felt instantaneous relief after reading his text.

"How did the breakup go?" Brandi asks while setting Genesis in her bouncer.

"Ken took it fairly well. He probably expected it since I texted him that we needed to talk."

"Ah, probably. Well, I'm glad it went okay."

"I invited your brother over for dinner tomorrow night," I tell Brandi.

"I know. He texted me," she says as a smile consumes her face. "Don't worry, Eva. He doesn't tell me everything about you two," she says and winks at me.

"Wait! What else did he tell you? Did he tell you about the dog pee and—and the dress?"

Brandi walks to her bedroom. "I'm going to take a nap before work. Goodnight!" She ignored me. Yeah, I'm pretty sure she knows details about the dog pee dress. Lovely.

Chapter Twenty-Three

An Afternoon with Grandma & Grandpa

Sunday, early afternoon, Genesis and I decide to spend some time over at my parents. My mom insisted on cooking us lunch, and the four of us are sitting around the dining room table. Genesis is the first one to be served, since she was impatiently waiting and screaming at the top of her lungs. She loves grandma's cooking, even more than mine. My mouth begins to water as my mom spoons a heaping mound of beef chow fun onto my plate.

"So, how's everything going with Ken?" my dad asks before taking a bite of his noodles.

"Um, well, I broke up with him… yesterday," I say, wincing at the thought of what is to come.

I knew my parents were going to ask me about Ken sooner or later, but the thought of disappointing them hurts my heart.

"Oh dear," my mom says. "What did you do?"

"What did *I* do?" I repeat, angrily. I was so offended my mom would even ask that.

"I'm sorry. I mean, what happened?" she corrects herself.

"Well, first of all, just to clarify—*I* didn't do anything," I explain, still frustrated. "I realized Ken wasn't the best option for Genesis and me."

My dad looks angry, and I watch as my mom wipes away a tear forming at the corner of her eye.

"So, tell us what happened," my dad demands. He wants more of an explanation.

"I don't know, Dad. I guess... I just wish Ken wanted to spend more time with Genesis. I also didn't like having to constantly wear nice outfits around him."

There is a long, awkward pause.

"Those dresses made you look like a streetwalker," my dad says, and my mom and I can't help but laugh.

"Yes, I know, Dad. They did," I say, agreeing with him.

"So, are you seeing Brian?" my mom asks. My parents are smarter and more observant than I give them credit for.

"Yeah," I smile. "He's so great with Genesis. She loves him a lot."

"Yes, your dad and I saw that at her birthday party,"

my mom says. "He's grown up to be a handsome man."

My parents are taking the news a lot better than I thought they would. I was expecting them to give me a lecture about financial stability or something along those lines.

"I'm actually cooking Brian dinner tonight over at Brandi's place," I tell them. "Genesis and I should probably get going soon." I grab some more chow fun with my chopsticks and finish off the large portion of rice noodles on my plate.

"Well, Dad and I are glad it's working out with Brian. You seem much happier than you have been in a long time, and your happiness is very important to your father and me." My mom's smile is warm. Now I know she approves, and if my dad is allowing my mom to talk for him, I'm pretty sure I have his approval as well.

"I love you guys," I tell my parents, which, sadly, is not something we say often enough in our culture. Today is the day that I have decided to make more of a verbal effort to let my parents know that I truly care for them and appreciate everything they have done for their granddaughter and me. "Thank you for supporting me in my decision. I obviously never want to disappoint you. I am truly blessed to have you both as parents."

"We love you too, daughter," my dad says, and once again, my plate is empty, and my heart is full.

Chapter Twenty-Four

Mr. Right

Brian picks the toy teapot off the floor and pours Genesis and himself a cup of tea. Genesis and Brian are thoroughly enjoying their tea party on the living room floor as I cook dinner. I am captivated, watching them play together. My daughter points to Brian's teacup while saying a couple words that are unrecognizable, telling him to take a sip. He lifts the plastic cup to his mouth and pretends to drink the tea. "Mmm, yummy!" he says to Genesis. She smiles at Brian, satisfied he has followed her demands.

Genesis picks up the fake chocolate chip cookie off her plate and chucks it across the room. It clanks loudly as it skips along the floor. She does the same thing with the plates as well as the teacups. Brian sets Genesis in her bouncer and hands my daughter her baby elephant. She is content and continues to give the stuffed animal endless hugs.

I pour soy sauce over the rice. "It smells ridiculously good in here," Brian says after he takes a whiff of the savory aroma that floats through the air.

"Yup, I'm almost finished," I tell him. Then, I add the oyster sauce, which helps give the fried rice a sweet flavor. Lastly, I sprinkle some roasted sesame seeds over the fried rice and give it one last stir before I turn the burner off.

"All right, dinner is done. I'm just going to change real quick, and then we can eat."

"You need to change?" he asks, confused as he bends over to pick up Genesis' tea set.

"Yes," I say before I walk into the bathroom.

I slip on the same red dress that I was wearing the night I had fallen into the dog pee. Well, okay, not the same exact dress. The day before our date at the aquarium, I had placed another online order for a new one. I hoped I would be able to wear a dress that wasn't saturated in dog pee for Brian.

I take a few minutes to curl my hair into flowy waves and put some make-up on. I walk out of the bathroom and over to Brian, who is now relaxing on the couch. I hover my body above Brian's and kiss him gently on his lips. Then I stand up and take a step back from the couch, so Brian can get a better look at my dress.

He sits up straight and asks, "Is that the same dress...?"

"Yup, but a size bigger and no dog pee," I say. We both start to laugh.

He leans forward, placing his elbows on each of his knees, and rests his chin on top of his fists. "You look gorgeous," he says as I spin around to provide a full view of my outfit. "You didn't have to get all dolled up for me, you know? If I would've known you wanted to dress all fancy tonight, I would've changed out of my tank top and cargo shorts." He leans back into the couch but doesn't take his eyes off me as I walk back into the kitchen to plate our fried rice.

"I know, but I wanted to do something nice for you besides cooking you dinner. I like your tank top and cargo shorts," I explain.

"Well, I can't complain," he says.

I smile at him. "Okay, well, I will have your fried rice ready to go in just a minute—fresh fried rice," I say.

"What's the difference?" he questions. He puts Genesis into her highchair, and she starts to whine, expecting something to eat.

"Uh, no difference actually, just tastes more... fresh." We both chuckle. "So, what movie did Genesis pick this time?" I ask.

225

"Oh, she picked, *A Walk to Remember*," he says as he starts the movie.

"How did you know that's my favorite—" I realize he had been texting Brandi again. The very first time I'd watched *A Walk to Remember*, I had fallen in love with Jamie and Landon's passionate relationship. I used to wonder if I would ever find someone as perfect for me like Landon did with Jamie.

"Brandi told me," he says with a proud smile.

I shake my head. "You and her. Oh, boy. I feel like you guys are constantly ganging up on me."

I bring over two bowls of fried rice to the living room and hand Brian his dinner. Before he takes a bite of his rice, he makes sure Genesis is content and gives her a generous portion out of his bowl.

"So, about our conversation on our last date—" Brian starts to say—"I'm sorry for just driving off." He looks disappointed in himself.

"It's really not your fault. I shouldn't have made that promise to you without breaking it off with Ken first," I say. "I ended up hurting both of you, and that wasn't cool. If it's any consolation... I told Ken we couldn't see each other anymore."

"You did?" Brian says, surprised.

"Yeah, I did. He wasn't the right fit for me and Genesis," I explain. "But I think I found *someone* who is."

I smile at Brian before taking a bite of my rice.

"I think I am too. I mean, I love spending time with both of you. I felt so disappointed after our conversation at the aquarium. The thought of never spending time with you and Genesis made me feel terrible."

I quickly swallow my mouthful of food and lean over to kiss Brian on his sensual lips. He grabs the back of my head and kisses me again.

After dinner, Brian helps with the dishes, and I read Genesis a book before putting her down for bed.

"I ordered us dessert," Brian says.

"You did? What did you order?" I ask, surprised.

"I ordered us each a Halo-halo," he says, smiling proudly.

"Oh my gosh! Brandi!"

"Yeah, she also told me that it's one of your favorite desserts," he explains. "I placed the delivery order for 8:00 p.m., though. I wasn't sure when we would be done with dinner."

"That's so thoughtful of you. I'm so excited! It's, literally, been over a month since I've had a Halo-halo," I say. "Have you had one before?"

"No, but I thought I would give it a try. If you like it, chances are I will like it too."

"You won't regret it. It's *the* best," I explain. "The purple yam is my favorite, and I love the coconut ice cream on top. It's the perfect combination." My mouth starts to water, thinking about all the goodness.

"That's exactly what I got you. My sister knows a lot about you," he says.

Brian brings me Genesis' bottle, and I rock her to sleep. He takes her from my hands and lays her down in her crib, takes her hearing aid out, and puts it in the case.

"You are becoming a pro," I say, jokingly, but deep down, I know I'm not joking at all because Brian really is becoming an amazing addition to our family.

Brian walks over to me and joins me on the couch. He reaches for the remote and turns off the TV. He holds my hand and tucks a wavy strand of hair behind my ear.

He looks into my eyes and says, "I know this might sound cheesy… but ever since you became friends with my sister, I've always pictured myself kissing you." Brian's eyes are dark like the deepest depths of the sea. I've never seen someone with such ravishing eyes. They are pure perfection. I give him a gentle kiss on his divine lips and lay my head on his shoulder. I place my hand on his firm chest. He puts his arm around me, and I find comfort in his warmth. Brian continues, "Even though we've only just started dating, I feel like I've been with you and Genesis for months, if not years."

"Okay… creeper," I say, sarcastically. I begin to

giggle at my joke, but then my laughing ceases as I look up and notice Brian staring at me.

"And this might sound insane, but… I think I might love you, Eva."

He tilts my chin up even higher and begins to kiss me passionately. I can feel his tongue gently graze my bottom lip. Brian tastes like clouds, harvested directly from Heaven. He runs his hands down the length of my body, enjoying every inch of me. He slides his hand under the hem of my dress and begins touching me in places I haven't been touched in a very long time. Flames crawl up my inner thighs, and my body ignites. His touch is like a drug, and my body is screaming for more.

I stand up and face Brian. I smile and slowly pull off my panties. I eagerly fling them onto the coffee table as Brian anxiously unzips his shorts. I straddle Brian, and he presses the back of his head into the couch. His eyes close, and my head tilts back as Brian firmly pulls thick strands of my wavy hair. He forces his eyes to open so he can slide the shoulder straps on my dress down my arms. His kisses tickle my neck. Brian works his way down farther to my chest, and then—the doorbell rings.

Brian throws himself against the back of the couch and tosses his hands up. "Oh, come on! The driver's here already?" He glances at his watch.

I laugh at his comment, and then I gently slide

myself off Brian's lap. "It's okay. I will just stick them in the freezer, and then we can continue where we left off." I pull the straps to my dress back over my shoulders. "Don't move. I will be right back," I tell Brian and bend over to kiss him before walking to the front door. A protective wiener dog follows me.

I open the door, expecting to see a delivery guy. "Oh, shit!" I say too loudly. I stand in front of Liam— hair ravaged and pantiless. He's holding a bouquet of red tulips. My eyes are bulging out of my skull and my lips are tightly pursed together.

He looks me in the eyes and says, "Hi, Eva. Do you have a minute to talk?"

Anxiety floods my body, and I can feel my muscles begin to stiffen. "Um, I—sure, but give me one second," I murmur and quickly shut the door, leaving Liam to wait outside.

My short legs double-time it to the living room. What could Liam possibly want to talk about? I haven't heard from him in over a year and a half. Multiple scenarios are running through my head.

"Everything okay?" Brian asks just as soon as I walk back into the room. He can see the panic spewed across my face.

"Um, Liam is at the door," I tell Brian. My eyes are still wide, and I think my body might be trembling a little bit from the fear of what Liam wants to talk about. I shake out my arms and hands, hopeful it will help calm my nerves.

"Oh, wow, okay," Brian says as he quickly stands up and zips up his shorts. "He just showed up unannounced?"

"Yeah, I haven't talked to him in over a year and a half," I explain. "I'm going to go ahead and let him in... I guess?"

I attempt to brush my sex hair out with my fingers before opening the door. Sasuke is barking uncontrollably, and his fur is furled along the top of his long spine. "Um, sorry to keep you waiting," I say to Liam. He now has the flowers tucked under his arm and is holding a carrier with Brian's and my shaved ice sundaes.

"Uh, I'"—Liam hands me the desserts—"the driver gave me these."

My fingers accidentally graze his hand during our exchange. Normally, I wouldn't apologize for something like that, but for whatever reason, I felt the need to. "Uh, sorry," I say and walk back to the living room. Sasuke is following Liam's feet, continuing to bark at the unknown person who has entered his domain. Liam's scent is unfamiliar to our guard dog. I run to the kitchen and place the desserts in the freezer, pick up Sasuke, and put him in the backyard before he decides to bite Liam.

"Um, did I interrupt something?" Liam says, uncomfortably. His eyes are going back and forth from Brian to the lacy thong I had thrown onto the coffee table a few minutes ago.

"Crap, sorry about that," I say to Liam, but I look at Brian. Brian looks just as frazzled and in shock as I do. I quickly grab my panties off the coffee table and toss them into the hamper I keep next to the couch. I try to slow my breathing and hide the fact that I'm slightly out of breath from running around in circles for the last two minutes.

I notice Liam look at Genesis sleeping in her crib. He sets down the bouquet of tulips and slowly walks over to her. He looks excited but scared and nervous at the same time. "Can I pick her up?" he asks me. "I know she's sleeping, but I just want to hold her for a minute."

"Um, well, she is your daughter," I say, giving him permission. "Maybe just try to pick her up slowly and try not to wake her up. She might stay asleep." I keep thinking of how uncomfortable I feel in this present situation.

Liam gently picks up his daughter from her crib. Her eyes open as she looks at her father for the first time. "Hi, Genesis," he says, hesitantly. "I'm sorry I woke you up and haven't stopped by sooner to see you."

I wonder if Liam's words are directed toward Genesis as well as me.

"Maybe, I should go," Brian says to me.

I firmly grab Brian's arm with both of my hands and hold him in place. "No, stay! Please!" I try to say quietly. His presence is the one thing that is making this uncomfortable moment bearable. I don't want to be alone with Liam. I haven't sorted out my feelings properly, and I don't know what I want to say to Liam just yet. There's a lot of tension in the room between the three of us.

Genesis starts to whimper and then screams while Liam holds her in his arms. Tears start to stream down her red cheeks as she reaches for Brian, begging him to hold her. Liam tries to bounce Genesis. He repeatedly bends his knees in strange ways—inexperienced and new. Genesis isn't soothed and continues to scream. I reach over and take her from Liam. Genesis' screams are now only small whimpers, but she is still traumatized from waking up in a stranger's arms.

"Maybe it might be better if we talk another day," I tell Liam.

"Yeah, sorry. I did show up unannounced, didn't I? I guess I will show myself out," Liam says, and he walks toward the door, defeated.

I decide to follow Liam and hand Genesis to Brian.

Genesis completely stops crying when she notices who is currently holding her. I catch Liam before he is able to step out the door. "I will call you tomorrow, okay?" I tell him. He nods and walks back to his car.

I think he might want Genesis to be a part of his life, and I would want that more than anything. I'm also scared because he left us when I was only four months pregnant. How would I find the strength to forgive something like that?

Brian had followed me to the door. He is still holding my daughter in his arms. Genesis looks sleepy but content. "I wouldn't have expected him to show up in a million years," I say to Brian. "I thought he wanted us out of his life for good."

The expression on Brian's face looks empathetic but also a little annoyed and concerned.

"You don't have to worry about Liam," I try to reassure Brian, but he doesn't say anything.

I urge him over to the couch. Before I sit down next to Brian and Genesis, I pick up the bouquet of tulips and throw them into the trash. I pull Brian's arm around my shoulders, and I nestle my head into his chest. Genesis is snuggled up against him as he cradles her in his other arm. I look at my daughter, and she giggles. Slowly but surely, her eyes close, and she falls back asleep.

I lift my head off Brian's chest, and our eyes

connect. I smirk at him and say, "You know… This might sound insane, but I think I might love you too. I think I have finally found Mr. Right." We smile at one another, and he passionately kisses me while he holds his two favorite girls in his arms.

To be continued

Thanks for reading my novel!

I would like to take the opportunity to thank you for your purchase. The support of each reader means everything to me. I hope you fell in love with Eva's story and are curious to find out what happens next in her life. If you enjoyed my novel, don't forget to leave a review. I would love to hear from you!

Keep in touch with me on social media—where you can learn more about the sequel to Fried Rice, giveaways, discounts, and future novels. I hope to chat with you soon!

Follow me on:

Facebook and Instagram @leahghermann

46818734R00142